Southpaw

by Dennis Sweeney

Order this book online at www.trafford.com
or email orders@trafford.com

Most Trafford titles are also available at major online book retailers.

Note for Librarians: A cataloguing record for this book is available from Library
and Archives Canada at www.collectionscanada.ca/amicus/index-e.html

Printed in Victoria, BC, Canada.

ISBN: 9781-4251-842-0-9 (soft)

ISBN: 9781-4251-842-1-6 (eBook)

*We at Trafford believe that it is the responsibility of us all, as both individuals
and corporations, to make choices that are environmentally and socially sound.
You, in turn, are supporting this responsible conduct each time you purchase a
Trafford book, or make use of our publishing services. To find out how you are
helping, please visit www.trafford.com/responsiblepublishing.html*

*Our mission is to efficiently provide the world's finest, most comprehensive
book publishing service, enabling every author to experience success.
To find out how to publish your book, your way, and have it available
worldwide, visit us online at www.trafford.com*

Trafford rev. 07/13/09

 www.trafford.com

North America & international
toll-free: 1 888 232 4444 (USA & Canada)
phone: 250 383 6864 ♦ fax: 250 383 6804 ♦ email: info@trafford.com

10 9 8 7 6 5 4 3 2 1

For Linda

_____

"Strike down with the sword of wisdom the ignorance that lies within and arise great warrior... arise."

Bagahvad Gita

_____

Table of Contents

PROLOGUE – BAN KWAN

I SIT HERE in prison trying to work out where it all went wrong. I suppose it's the force of circumstances, or Karma. Bad Karma. Officer Sonchai told me that. He's a prison guard on death row. He's a Buddhist. I mean they're all Buddhists but Sonchai seems to practice what he preaches. A lot of this Buddhist stuff is alien to the Western mind, all this Karma and reincarnation business, it might even seem odd for us to contemplate the reason for our existence. I never actually thought about it until I got sentenced to thirty seven and a half year's jail for possession of heroin. Even some of my family back in Scotland think I deserve to die in prison, or even worse. I suppose anyone daft enough to smuggle smack in Thailand is asking for trouble. There is no remission or time off for good behavior, so I'll be fucking seventy five years old when I get out of here. If I survive that long.

Then again, I don't mind the idea that I can continue to participate in the evolutionary process until I get it right, because these allotted three score years and ten have been one almighty fuck-up so far. In the eyes of the Thai correction department my crime is worse than any other. In this prison there are people who have committed the most heinous crimes against humanity. Sister killers. Mother rapists. Baby eaters. All eligible for amnesties and parole. But because four new members of the Thai parliament were refused US visas for their known drug involvement, the Thai government decided to 'get tough' on drugs and excluded drug offenders from the amnesties.

So it looks like I'm here for the duration. The finite in me is damned. But the *Judeo-Christian* belief that I will burn in Hell for eternity doesn't appeal to me. When I do eventually cast off this mortal coil, I like the idea that I can come back and try again. I have seen the Evangelist *Christian* 'God Squad' at work in here, telling sinners to get on their knees and beg forgiveness from the man in the clouds with the beard. I just can't relate to that shit man, it's too depressing. I'm fucking sorry enough. This prison is full of the sorriest cunts on earth, and I don't want to be beating myself up anymore than I have to. The *Buddhists* believe that you're punished *'by'* your sins not *'for'* them. I was greedy. Now I'm being punished. End of fucking story.

1

HAYFOOT STRAWFOOT

MY FATHER HAD a boxing club in Dundee, and some of my earliest memories are of having my little, soft, newly formed head punched in. My father and the other trainers would demonstrate till they were blue in the face. Left, left, left, right was the correct method of punching the bag, but I couldn't even get that. I liked to go right, right, and right, left. They tried to correct me but I was clearly a hopeless case, a complete non-starter. I couldn't get my head around the conventional orthodox approach, which was the left hand lead for the jab, then big right hand for the knock-out punch. My right hand was my jab and also my hardest punch. It seemed an impossible task to co-ordinate all these movements simultaneously. The feet had to dance, the hands had to punch and the head and body had to bob and weave. Then there was the noise thing you're supposed to make every time you throw a punch. I would always forget the noise or do it too late, long after I had thrown the punch. The nose-noise was very important according to my father and I had to get it right!

I was dumpy and was one of those kids who just couldn't seem to get it together; bad coordination I suppose. My brother Tony, on the other hand, was a natural athlete. He had a long left-handed reach and good compact shoulders. He was tall and slim for his age and could float like a butterfly on his little feet. I could sense the disappointment in my father's eyes when we were at the boxing club. I was a bit slow on the uptake and for some odd reason seemed incapable of defending myself. "Two left feet!" they used to say. The biggest problem was when we got into the ring to spar; that's when my lack of the basic fundamentals of pugilism would show through and I would get my arse kicked publicly, sorely humiliating my poor father! Every time I got in the ring the same scenario would be repeated. Whoever my opponent was, he would rush me with a flurry of punches and I would end up on the floor, bringing shame on everyone including myself and a curse on the good name Sweeny, which had a long line of national champions behind it. My uncle Frank represented his country fifty times; what an honour it was to fight for Scotland, '*Scotland the Brave!*' My uncle Danny was Scottish team captain and runner-up in the British championships and my father had four hundred fights under his belt. Dad was the giant-killing captain of the British team, nicknamed the '*Lion of Bucharest*' for his outstanding victory in Hungary against Laslo Flapp, the only communist ever to be allowed to turn pro. Then there was me, a little *tub'o'lard* who couldn't even throw his left hand first.

What made it worse was that even at home, if someone came round to visit, my brother Tony would be asked to demonstrate his prowess. He would dance around the living room, throwing left jabs and right crosses, going "*mhew! mhew!*" with every punch. Everybody had their own kind of "*mhew*" noise but Tony tried to copy Jimmy Douglas who was British champion and, therefore, had the loudest "*mhew*" in the club. It was a bit like going to church where it was always the wankers who sing and pray the loudest. Now I'm not saying that Jimmy Doug-

4

las was a wanker; he was a great champion and would have won the gold medal at the Montreal Olympics in 1976 if he hadn't been punched in the solar plexus by some Korean tosser. I know the solar plexus is technically within the scoring area but it's unethical to aim deadly *Kung Fu* blows in boxing.

I came to realise in later years that developing this re-lease of breath was essential to accentuate the power of a punch, but try telling that to wee boys in their string vests striving to imitate champions. My older brother would annoy me, standing in front of the mirror in all his finery practicing the *nose-noise*. The expulsion of air from his nodule was extremely loud, due to the sheer length of his neb. His snotterbox was enormous and his pen-chant for snow-sledging and hairy anoraks earned him the moniker of '*The Jewish Eskimo*'. He certainly looked like one of God's frozen people.

I hated going to the boxing club. It was demean-ing and soul-destroying as everybody and their mother knew I was the son of the great champion.

"Oh, yir father's the boxer... Oh, I've seen yir father on the TV... What a great fighter yir father is, son... Oh what a great father yir father is! And you, son? Do you box? You must be a natural."

Then there was my younger brother Danny; same whiskey different bottle. Danny had a long reach and was light on his feet, a natural athlete who took to box-ing like a fish to water. I think I may have been a slow starter or a maybe a late developer, but Danny was like one of those day-old calves that come galloping out of the womb and hit the ground running. It was his coordi-nation. Some people are born with it. I obviously wasn't, but that's not to say you can't train for it. I mean, it's like how most of the farmers *(teuchters)* in Scotland were taught Scots' country dancing. As they couldn't tell their left foot from their right, the teacher would put a bit of hay on one foot and a bit of straw on the other and instead of saying *left foot, right foot,* they would say *hay foot, straw foot.* Danny and Tony already knew their *hay feet* from their *straw feet.*

I was really getting fed up with being the laughing stock of the boxing club. Tony and Danny would be given all the attention on the bag work, the ring work and the combination work, whilst my father would give me an old skipping rope and tell me to *shadow skip* in the corner. I had heard of *shadow boxing,* where you stand in front of the mirror making the "mhew, mhew" noises and faking punches with a serious face on, but I didn't know what *shadow skipping* was. I did it anyway. I think he just wanted to get me out of the way so the real men could get on with the job in hand. Often he would send me into the woods to play hide-and-seek, but after a while I realised that nobody would ever come look for me.

2

WOOLY WOOFTER

EVENTUALLY MY FATHER decided to send me to my grandfather's house for private boxing lessons. It was a disgrace to have the fat one there in the corner of his club; shadow skipping, then getting belted all over the ring by any little mug that felt like it. Political correctness was yet to raise its ugly head in this neck of the woods; here people were as yet unafraid to call gardening implements by their proper name and rather than see me for what I was, a differently-abled child, my father said I was a hopeless little fat bastard. It wasn't that I was soft or anything; I just wasn't a natural born killer. So now after school, instead of getting my tea, it was up to my grandfather's for a toughening-up session. Granda would put a pair of boxing gloves on me, kneel down in front of me and tell me to punch him on the nose.

"I dinna want tae hurt yi Granda."

"How could a wee bliddy *Jessie* like you hurt anybody? Now dae as yir telt an' hit me."

"But I dinna want tae hit yi Granda."

He started slapping me in the face, screaming at me to hit him back, but I wasn't capable; couldn't see the point. I just stood there crying while he got his knickers in a right old twist, belting me all over the house.

"C'mon ya wee bliddy *Jessie Annie!* Have a go for God's sake."

He was really pissed off now and dragged me through to the kitchen by my hair, which he said was far too long for a boy and that I looked and acted like a wee lassie. Read; poof, homo, girly-boy.

"You canna be seen galavantin' roond the toon wi hair like a lassie."

The hair had to go before he would give me lessons in being a man, and not the *wee bliddy Jessie* that I was. My grandfather was ancient, or at least appeared to be, and his idea of how a young laddie's hair should look lent itself to Victorian images of street urchins, well-spanked scullery maids and skinny little skeletons stuck up lums, twirly moustaches, top hats and roars of "On-wards and upwards coachman! And don't spare the fuckin horses!" But who was I, a *Jessie* with two left feet, to argue. He brushed the cobwebs off these blunt, rusty old scissors and started hacking away at my locks. When that was done he brought out the *'machine'* as he called it. It had scissor-like legs but the cutting bit was some weird contraption not unlike a lawnmower of the hand held variety. One hand hacked with the blunt scissors while the machine tore into my head wrenching bits of scalp and hair onto the floor. If this was an initiation ceremony to manhood I was quite happy being a great big *Jessie Annie*, thank you very much!

I was standing there rubbing my sore head and feeling like a skinned rabbit when Granda produced a package from the cupboard. It was the kilt that I had worn in my old cross-dressing days. Although not much of a pugilist, I had apparently been a real show-off in my preschool years and loved wearing a kilt. I would perform my interpretation of the *Highland Fling* for anyone who was interested. Of course this aptitude to cross-dress was put down to childish folly and as soon as school started the kilt was *oot the windae*, the *troozers were on* and I was getting my haircut like a man!

"Pit it on, poofboy!"

"But Granda! It's too wee! A'hm a big boy noo!"

My tearful protestations were met with a swift clip around the ear. I had taken a bit of a stretch since the last time I had worn it and so it had now become more like a mini-kilt and barely reached my thighs. Now fully attired in my highland regalia, Granda delivered the *coup de grace* - a ribbon! Not just any old ribbon, may I add, but a great big fuck-off yellow and red polka-dot affair! There was barely enough hair to tie this monstrosity on, so he had to squeeze my head between his legs while he knotted this huge bow onto what little hair there was left on top of my scalp.

"Now, git roond to the shops and git me a newspaper. There's a bonny wee *Jessie*," he said endearingly, as he booted my arse out the door. I desperately tried to undo the knot on the wretched ribbon but it was too tight. The shops were at the other end of the housing scheme. I tried to cover the ribbon with my hands but it was too big. The taunts started almost immediately. My Granda's neighbours, the Murchies, shouted out the window.

"Oh, what a bonny lassie! What a braw ribbon!"

The adults' comments were unkind but still within the bounds of humour; kids are far more cruel.

"Oi, tart feautures! Show's yir arse! Geez a feel oh yir tits! Mon ower here hen and ah'll slip ye a crippler."

When I got round to the shops there was a big gang of boys hanging around. In Dundee, the worst possible insult to a young male would be to suggest that he was on a *different bus*. Scottish men can be deeply anal about homosexuality. The old saying goes that in Dundee if you're intellectual then you're homosexual and if you can SPELL homosexual then you must fucking BE one. Here was I, a wee *Jessie* with a big ribbon and a tartan skirt on; a prime target for their virulent pent up *Jessiephobia*.

They had sticks and started hitting me with them. I was getting skelped from every direction with the sticks, and to be honest, I was getting a bit fed up of being used as a punching-bag by anyone who felt like it, so I got stuck in and retaliated. I managed to grab hold of one of them by the hair. Somebody hit me in the back of the legs and I fell down but I was still holding on to this kid's hair so I brought him down with me. I was smashing his face into the pavement while the other kids battered me with their sticks. It all got a bit like a feeding frenzy until Luigi, the Italian bloke who owned the chip shop, came out and pulled them off.

I got back to my Granda's house and gave him the newspaper. He looked disapprovingly at my bruises and bloodied nose.

"Did ye hae a wee bit o' barney rubble son?"

"Och ay the noo, Granda, but it's alright. I gied thon lassies blouse a good belt in his north and sooth. "

That was it. From that day on my grandfather started to actually teach me how to box. He didn't try to correct my stance. He said I was fine with my right, right, and right, left. I was a *southpaw*, he told me, and Dick McTaggart, who was also a *southpaw*, was the finest boxer Scotland had ever produced. My Granda may have been old but he had produced three national champions of his own so he knew his onions, even though his methods may have seemed a little off-centre.

My main problem was coordinating my feet; I just couldn't dance. My punches were quick and solid, and now that they had all stopped trying to correct my stance from *southpaw* to *orthodox*, I was coming on a storm. My Granda started demonstrating the footwork for a boxer. He wasn't exactly nimble on his feet, as he had been in a mining accident at the age of twenty and had spent most of his adult life on crutches. It must have looked strange to the neighbours to see this old man, who they thought of as a cripple, skipping around the back green showing his mincey grandson some fancy footwork.

After about a month of this intensive training my Granda declared I was ready. I had now learned the footwork. "Punching is a natural instinct," he would say, "it's the footwork that has to be learned." He proudly marched me up to the club after school, where my dad and the other trainer looked at me with a cross between pity and despair. I wasn't feeling too sure about this myself. After all, training is one thing and we can all look like Muhammed Ali in front of the mirror, but when it comes to stepping into the ring it's a different story altogether.

Frazer Ormond was my first opponent; he was shorter than me and a right stocky little bastard. When I had boxed him before, he had always rushed me with two hands and beat me to the floor in a flurry of punches. The bell went and Frazer rushed me with his usual tactics but now I had the footwork. I pivoted to the right and parried his wild haymakers with my steady jab. A few straight rights to the nose took the wind out of his sails, and by the time I hit him with a big left he was begging for mercy. He ran out of the ring, didn't want to know. My father and the other trainer looked on in disbelief as my grandfather beamed down at me.

Next up was Wullie Carr. He had used me as a punchbag so many times it wasn't funny. There was something about his awkward stance that I hadn't been able to get my head around. My Granda had worked out a combination especially for Carr and it worked like magic. I extended my reach to parry his jab, crossed my left hand and sank it into his face. Wullie dropped to his knees and started crying so they took him out of the ring. While the two lads went to wash the blood off their noses, my father praised me and patted me on the head and held out his open palms so I could repeat the winning combination on his hands. What a wonderful feeling of acceptance! I could do it. I could fight!

3

MANUFACTURING CONSENT

BEING A CLEVER child, I didn't really mind school-work. My parents suggested studying medicine but the teacher said it wasn't possible to write prescriptions with spray cans. Crime wasn't really an option though because career criminals in Dundee were so skint they had to do drive-by shootings from the bus. The only careers that were on offer were more of the plumber, brickie, fitter, welder variety; and that was only if you were lucky. The town was full of what would now be described as dysfunctional families, but the want, quarrel and debt lay so heavily upon my little community that I am now of the opinion that it was the system that was dysfunctional. Most people were merely ashamed of their poverty instead of being angry at the political system that had marginalized them. But rather than tell those political fuck-wits to go and get real jobs, they kept voting them into power.

Our street bully was a formidable lard-bucket who went by the name of Slug McGlashan. He was one nasty, evil, bullying thug. Not only did this guy eat worms, he would swallow big fat slugs in one go. He always had a stick with a nail in it and wouldn't think twice about giving you a whack with it. Now you can call me an arse-licker, a brown-noser or whatever, but if you weren't in Slug's gang you were in trouble. There were a few boys in the street whose mothers had told them not to play with Slug, and boy did they suffer. Slug was like a minia-ture *Michelin Man* with a face on him like a greasy ham-burger. Tying bangers to cats' tails and the like was the norm for Slug, and the old "I'll tell your father" routine didn't work with him like it did with the rest of us. Slug told us his father had died in police *'custardy'*. I never knew what *'custardy'* was, and I didn't want to ask Slug in case he hit me with his stick. I had images of police-men throwing Slug's father bound and gagged into a steaming vat of boiled custard.

Slug had three older brothers but they were all in a mental hospital. Sometimes they would get out for a few days, but Slug's mum would beat them so hard they would be glad to get back in there. Slug was a holy ter-ror that was for sure. My father was always telling us off for hanging about with him, and he couldn't quite get his head round the fact that the reason we hung about with him was because we were scared not to. My fa-ther's advice would be to give him a *good punch on the nose*. That may have been all right for the *'Lion of Bucharest'*, but the only time I tried that tactic on Slug he nearly killed me. It was like punching a greasy space-hopper.

There was one wee boy called John Sinclair who lived on the top floor of our tenement. He had a nice clean school uniform and two lovely sisters with posh voices. His parents had told him that he wasn't allowed to talk to Slug. One day Slug and the posse, including a reluctant me, hijacked John Sinclair with sticks and forced him around to a patch of waste ground at the end of the street where there was a big anthill that Slug made Sinclair stand upon. While we all surrounded the poor wee bugger with sticks in hand, Slug began to prod the anthill, aggravating the ants that in turn started to crawl up Sinclair's legs. He started to cry and when he tried to move off the anthill, Slug hit him over the head with the stick. We were all told by Slug to point our sticks, kidding us on that they were swords and aiming them at Sinclair so he couldn't move. Sinclair was sobbing desperate tears, which made the evil Slug even happier so responded by hitting him between the eyes with the blunt end of his stick.

"Drap yir breeks and shite yi wee poof!"

Sinclair did what he was told and dropped his kecks and squatted down for a poop. He was crying so much that he could hardly breathe, but Slug kept prodding him with the stick.

"Shite, yi wee poof! Shite!"

The ants were now biting Sinclair's arse and legs as he desperately tried to curl one. Eventually he made a run for it and the poor little mite was hysterical as he ran away with the skitters running down his legs, tripping over his trousers with ants crawling and biting him everywhere. Slug loved that incident and being quite the raconteur; it was to become one of his favourite after dinner stories.

Things were quite tough then. Some people might say we had it hard but I still remember many fun-filled evenings around at Slug's house in the candlelight (the electricity was always cut off) listening to Slug's riotous, ribaldous repartee. The ants would be bigger, the shite smellier and Sinclair's scrunties mair be-skidded. Lang may his bum reek.

4

BARON VON BEEHIVE

SLUG'S NEIGHBOURS DIDN'T like him, for obvious reasons, and so by way of payback, someone grassed up his Mum for having a hairdressing salon in her coal cupboard. The makeshift salon was a wee cupboard-like affair at the back of the house, with just enough room in it for two fat ladies (click, click, click) and a chair. However, Slug's mum had painted her coal cupboard lime green and put mirrors inside so the local women could come around and have their hair done. The beehive was the in-thing at the time. To tell the truth that particular style of haircut didn't really suit your average Dundee housewife, who tended to be short and round, mainly due to a staple diet of fried Mars Bars, porridge and chips. These very large hairdos accentuated their rotundity, making them somewhat resemble the reflections seen in a funfair hall of mirrors. Fleshy underarms, or bingo wings as we used to call them, were also much in evidence. These short, fat but happy suburban wifies would sit around drinking buckets of tea and chain-smoking their Woodbines.

One night Slug's neighbour, Granny McGurk, was staggering home pissed from the pub. We called him Granny cause he was always moaning and continually ranted and raved about the Germans when he was wasted. Granny said he'd been in the *Black Watch,* which had been the first regiment over the Rhine River during the war. The Scots were *first in and last oot* in every fracas according to Granny. This night that Granny was staggering home, we (the gang) were in Slug's garden and music was blaring out of the open windows. It couldn't have been that late because the pubs shut about nine thirty in those days. As Granny staggered past he shouted.

"Oi you, ya wee fat cunt! Turn that music doon or I'll put my boot up your fuckin arse!"

As the final word came out of his mouth, Slug's mum and some of her entourage from the drinking men's club appeared from around the corner, all looking like escapees from *Diddyland*.

"You lay a finger on my wee laddie and I'll rip your bloody head aff, McGurk, you auld bugger!" Slug's mum bellowed.

Granny McGurk made a run for it and managed to bolt his front door with Mother McGlashan and her mates in hot pursuit. As the others were kicking at his door, Mrs McGlashan was shouting up at his window.

"Ye widnae be sae lippy if my man wiz alive you auld nonce! Pickin on wee laddies that's aw yir good fir!"

McGurk hung out his window.

"Awa, and fuck yersel's! And git awa fae ma door or I'll phone the polis! That's not a wee laddie, that's a wee monster and he'll end up like heez father. Locked up in the jail whaur he belongs."

Mrs McGlashan burst into tears. "You leave the laddie's father oot oh this!"

McGurk closed his window and everything settled down.

Nobody quite knew for sure who it was that grassed up Mrs McGlashan and her little hairdressing salon business, but it seemed pretty obvious to me.

17

The following morning the people from the dole office came round and started taking pictures of Mrs McGlashan's coal bunker and charged her with illegally using it for clandestine *beehive* production. Flagrant abuse of the legal system of this magnitude did not amuse the judge and Mrs McGlashan was duly fined fifty pounds. In addition, her dole was stopped for a whole month and she was forced to shut down the coal bunker. It was quite a big case back then and I clearly remember the headlines in the paper .

"Beehive Baron Milks Welfare State!"

Her *beehive* industry still carried on in spite of the judgment, only a little more on the hush-hush than before. Instead she continued her illicit *beehive* production in the bedroom with the blinds down. The women would wear sunglasses and scarves over their *beehives* when leaving the house just in case they were photographed by the dole. They needn't have worried; the government didn't really consider her a threat and the media bloodhounds had already had their day. It was not Mrs McGlashan that was bringing the government to its knees, but rather the sixteen-year-old lassies who were purposefully getting pregnant with the sole intention of procuring council houses. There was talk of compulsory neutering of all lassies on benefits or lower incomes but it hasn't happened. Not yet anyway.

5

BLUE PETER

ONE INCIDENT IN particular sent McGurk over the edge; it was the straw that broke the camel's back, so to speak. On this particular day Slug made us go around collecting dog shite. He insisted that the texture had to be soft, runny and it also had to pass the smell test. Like a trained army we took to our tasks with the dicipline of professional soldiers. Aye, t'was a shit job richt enough but somebody had to do it. It wasn't the first time we had performed this operation and we all knew the procedure. The gathering of runny keech is more complicated than the picking up of a solid stool but runny keech was definitely the superior product, whiff-wise at least. Our fearless leader had come prepared and dramatically presented each of us with a clothes peg for our noses. "Go forth and multiply," bellowed the stout Slug as we scattered to the far corners of the scheme in search of bounty. We would hold our offerings up to Slug for inspection and he would poke at the shite to make sure it was runny enough. Then he would ask my brother Tony to give it the sniff test, because the Jewish Eskimo's olfactory senses were much more enhanced, and after a hefty sniff of each individual offering he would either give it the thumbs up or dismiss it with a theatrical wave of the hand. He would savour each sniff like a true connoisseur before pronouncing the final judgment. Eventually we would get the winning recipe. Isn't it weird how some turds are odourless and some absolutely ming to buggery?

Anyway, we took our excrement collection over to McGurk's in a bucket and put a sheet of newspaper on the ground just outside his front door. Then we poured the runny keech, all over the base and interlaced sheet upon sheet of newspaper. It was a bit like making a *Blue Peter* papier-mache model.

"Children, ask your parents to dig out the toilet bowls and spread them over today's *Sun*. Like this model I made earlier."

When the mix was about two inches thick, we covered it with another couple of sheets of newspaper. I am trying to think of a way to describe just how bad this smelled. It was worse than a stink; it was more like poisonous gas! It was foul! If there had been any UN weapons inspectors around, we would have got nicked for producing chemical bombs. We then crumpled up a load of newspapers and spread them over the top. The shite was now invisible to the human eye.

Our fearless leader then told us to make ourselves scarce while he triumphantly set fire to a torch made from newspaper. He waved the blazing torch above his head as he banged on the door shouting "Come and git it McGurk, you auld cunt, yir fuckin teas oot!"

He dropped the blazing torch on the pile of newspapers interlaced with shite and made a dash for it. Our unsuspecting victim came running out in his undies and slippers with a toothbrush hanging out his mouth. He saw the burning newspaper outside his door and started jumping on the fire to put it out. The shite squelched in every direction, splattering his door and walls. Eventually the poor man slipped over arse first, with arms and legs waving frantically like a drowning man, and every last scrap of dignity he had went with him as he plunged deep into the shite! The following day the men in the white coats drove up in their green van with square wheels and whisked him away to the funny farm. His anguished pleas could be heard clearly throughout the street as he was manhandled into a straightjacket and bundled into the back of the van.

"The Queen's a German! They're all bliddy Germans! Bliddy House of Hanover Nazi German bastards!"

His patriotic song was muffled as the green van closed its barred doors and the square wheels began to turn.

6

COME THE REVOLUTION

STATISTICS HAVE PROVEN that due to socio-economic conditions, Scottish children are likely to be fatter, smellier, thicker and more prone to violence than children in other parts of Britain. When I was a child, my Granda would fill my head with first hand accounts of when he was six years old; doing eighteen hour factory shifts and walking barefoot in the snow to get to work. My other Granda, a Derry man, terrified me with stories of how the Black and Tans burned their villages and raped their women.

My father was a shop steward, an atheist and a communist all in one. He totally rejected the whole 'wage slave' concept, as he called it, and would not approve of anything in the constituted order of things.

It was pretty much destined for me which side of the fence I was to sit on; my peers had done an excellent job on my young impressionable mind and their nihilism had left its mark. Dundee would never offer me more than a life of working class mediocrity. It was a *Them and Us* scenario and *They* were definitely out to get me. The difficult thing was working out who *They* actually were. First, there were the obvious ones, your general run-of-the-mill servants of the state; policemen, teachers, priests and so forth. But these twats could be kept at arms length with a doff of the cap and "*a thank you very much indeed your holiness for that crust of bread, we are not worthy"* kind of attitude. *They* were too stupid to be a threat.

There were far more subtle forces at work here. The ones who controlled our minds. To protect myself from these unseen forces I developed a technique of psychological freedom fighting. I was certain the English were partly to blame although I knew deep down that the forces were on a larger, more international scale. So I set up a committee in my head, taking my model from the *McCarthy witch-hunters* of the fifties, and called my boys the *House of UnScottish Activities*. Cleanliness begins at home, so first person to fall under the finger of suspicion was my poor mother. She hailed from Edinburgh and her anglicised vowel sounds placed her dangerously close to that bourgeois category *'The Powers That Be'*. However, I knew that come the revolution, I would plead her case before the *House*; after all she was and always would be my ma. My mother was the daughter of a lowly builder; her cultural aspirations sprang from her love of books, and not as the *House* accuses, from being *To the Manor Born*; whilst the male members of her family died on the killing fields of Europe to stop the advancing Hun (actually they were fighting Britannia's Huns on the Fenian side of the Liffey but what the *House* doesn't know won't harm it).

"This waif of the blitz found her solace in knowledge; through air raids, rationing, rickets and scurvy, a hungry mite devouring literature by candlelight in place of food. In condemning this woman's actions as unScottish, we condemn our nation to an eternity of ignorance and, if the pursuit of knowledge is to be regarded as unScottish, then I put it you gentlemen, that you yourselves do not have Scotland's best interests at heart. I accuse the members themselves of being, not only unScottish, but dis-Scottish and even anti-Scottish."

I myself would bravely bare my neck to the executioners axe.

"*Les Enfant de la Patria, Ecrasez l'infamme. J'ai Accusse, j'ai accuse, j'ai accuse...*"

"*Up the wurkers... Break doon the barriers... Punch the fuck oot the fuzz... Let them eat porridge...*" and what have you. "*United we stand... blah, blah, blah... One out all out... Tits oot fir the boys.*"

7

TIN PAIL

THE REST OF my childhood passed without much con-
troversy, and due to my grandfather's patient tutelage
I became a formidable boxer in my early teens, winning
district and national championships. Shortly after my sixteenth birthday, the results came through for my "O"
level preliminary exams; I achieved six good passes and
was a dux in English with eighty-seven per cent. Definitely university material with marks like that, and I must admit to being a little bit chuffed with myself. I had never
met anyone who had been to university apart from my
teachers at school. People in my immediate environment were more likely to face the hell-holes of prison
than go in for higher education. "Not for the likes of us"
was the depressing mantra of the lumpen proletariat.

At about the same time I won the *Junior Welterweight
Championship* of Scotland, and was picked to represent
my country at the up-and-coming *Junior Olympics* in
Tokyo, Japan. All aspects of my life seemed incredibly
positive. The Scottish national soccer team had a play-
off game against Wales. It was to take place in Liverpool
and the anticipated result was that we would qualify for
the world cup in Argentina. Tickets were like gold but
my dad, through his sporting connections, managed
to procure one for me. I set off on match day by train,
which was packed with drunken hooligans going to the

football. I wasn't drinking at the time as I was training for the *Junior Olympics*, so by the time the train got to Liverpool I had had enough of drunk and violent football fans. There's nothing worse than being surrounded by piss-heads when you have to stay sober.

Fights were breaking out everywhere on the train. Scottish fans fuelled by drink fought with the police, train guards, ticket collectors and of course, each other. Scots don't really need a reason for a punch-up. The way they see it, *if ye cannae fight it, drink it or fuck it,* then you had best ignore it!

We, that is me and a few mates, arrived at Liverpool Station and hung around for a few hours. Just like the train, every pub was full of Scottish fans causing trouble. They were smashing up shitty little pubs and beating up unfortunate *Scouse* publicans. It was around five o'clock and the evening was closing in, so we started walking towards the football ground, minding our own business. We must have been quite close as the noise of the crowd could be clearly heard. We were walking down a residential street along with a couple of thousand other fans when a riot broke out. Drunken thugs began to trash the street, smashing windows and car windscreens. One guy even broke off a garden gate and put it through somebody's window.

We started to run but the *old bill* blocked of the street with a couple of paddy wagons. Some *Scouse* cunt from the smashed-up street came running towards us screaming "It was the bastard with the flag on." He was referring to the Scottish flag draped over my shoulders. I was bundled into the back of the meat-wagon, taken to Walton police station and made to sit in line with all the other fans who had been arrested. It was actually quite a jovial atmosphere in the police station, with all these pissed-up wankers laughing and joking with the pigs, but

I was livid. I was going to miss the match and the fuckin' train home.

We appeared before the Judge next morning. In all, there were ninety-nine Scots arrested, and one Welshman. The Scots all gave *Taffy* a big cheer when his name came up. He looked as though he was nursing a serious hangover. The Judge fancied himself as a bit of a comic and he asked each of the accused how much money they had on them at the time of their arrest. He then fined the victims of justice according to the amount of money they possessed, leaving each one with a solitary pound note to get home. He didn't seem like a bad bloke actually, because he didn't want to put anyone behind bars; he probably just wanted these barbaric heathens to go back up north where they belonged.

The other lads in the remand cell had suggested that I plead guilty. If I did then I would probably be fined and allowed to go home. The thing that worried me about pleading guilty was getting a criminal record, and that I wouldn't be allowed to go to Tokyo with the boxing team. So I pleaded not guilty; after all, I hadn't fuckin' done anything. The result of this was that the Judge set a date for the following month, which meant I would have to come back in Liverpool for the trial.

A month later my father drove me down to Liverpool. He was really pissed-off and convinced that I had brought this upon myself. A friend who had been at the match accompanied us; he was going to testify that this was a case of mistaken identity. The trial was a complete farce however, as half the people in the street testified against me. In typical Liverpudlian style, They were all trying to milk the system for as much compensation as possible. The reason there are no *Scousers* in *Star Trek* is because they don't want to work in the future either. About eight of these mingy looking housewives lined up as witnesses and swore blind that it was definitely me who smashed their windows and cars. Lying toe rags!

Six policemen took the stand and testified against me, stating that they had apprehended me in the act of causing criminal damage. The *plods* were straight out of a cartoon, helmet in one hand and notebook in the other. They all read their scripts without ever looking up from their notes.

"Your 'onour, I h'apprehended the h'accused after 'aving chased him for a considerable period of time."

Although numerically correct their *'aitches* were somewhat misplaced. The Judge eyed me with contempt. Somebody's head would roll for these crimes and it was my head on the chopping block. I took the stand and pleaded my innocence, but even the *Pope* would have been found guilty with so much incriminating evidence against him.

My lawyer tried to help my case by pointing out that I would have had to be some kind of *superman* to have systematically broken every window and car windscreen in the street. And how come the eye witnesses managed to identify me on such a dark night from thousands of other fans? They had obviously all collaborated on this story as every one of them, when questioned, said that they saw me wearing a Scottish flag. My lawyer then asked one of the star witnesses whether she was an expert on *'something-flag-ology'*. Even the Judge himself had to ask for a dictionary, as he didn't understand the meaning of this word either. It turned out to mean the study of flags, and the star witness admitted that no, she didn't really know one flag from another.

The most obvious, glaring inaccuracy in all of their stories was the question of where these people happened to be standing while I systematically smashed every window in the street. If they had been in front of their windows then the bricks would have hit them straight in the gob. For the amount of compensation these people were claiming you would think it had been smart bombs that had come through their windows. Not only did the front windows get smashed, but also these missiles seemed to take the exact same route in every household; apparently bouncing off walls, breaking videos, stereos and perhaps a hairdryer or two into the bargain. As if things weren't bad enough, I was also personally responsible for showering sleeping babies with broken glass and wounding old grannies. The case was cut-and-dried as far as the Judge was concerned. I was Scottish, so therefore I must be a vicious thug and a hooligan. I was only sixteen years old, but the old beak's eyes showed no mercy as he sentenced me. I was going to *Borstal* for two years; the most feared *short-sharp-shock* juvenile punitive regime in the British legal system. They knew how to deal with football hooligans in *Borstal*, and I would be made to repay my debt to society with two years of army-style boot camp, shaved heads, marching on the spot, cleaning toilets with toothbrushes and other such meaningless toss. Boot camps don't deter crime but they do turn out fitter criminals.

I waved goodbye to my dad as they led me down into police custody. I know he was scared too, although he wouldn't show it. I felt the fear eating away at my insides as they banged the cell door closed.

8

TEA LEAFS

AFTER EIGHTEEN MONTHS of sheer physical and mental torture, especially because I was the only Scot in a prison full of Scousers, they released me into mainstream society. I had been caged like an animal, branded as a criminal and hounded like a wolf. As a result, one can well imagine that my social tendencies were now somewhat mal-adjusted, and the urge to take out some heavy-duty societal beefs was tremendously strong. Two promises were made to myself when I came out of nick. One was never to work again, and the other was to take up where I had left off, by having sex with as many women as physically possible.

Back in Dundee, I started hanging out with a bunch of older, hardened, drug-dealing criminals whom I had met through the nepotistic old-boy prison network. They were known as the *Lucky For Some* gang and had all served time for an abortive blag when thirteen of them were caught trying to hold up a bank. Rumour had it that the lead gunman at the time of the robbery was dyslexic and had rushed into the bank waving his shotgun screaming "Hands up mother-stickers this is a fuckup!"

The leader's name was Ogerman or Ogie for short. He was a ginger-headed giant of a man with hands like shovels and a face like a well skelped arse. He was in the habit of carving his initials into the face of anyone who ran up drug debts with him. His first name was Billy so there quite a number of unfortunate *fizzogs* in Dundee decorated with the initials 'BO'. It was actually a fitting moniker for the ginger giant because if you stood down wind of him he hummed like a gorilla's armpit. These were cruel, heartless, evil fuckers, who didn't believe in taking prisoners! We would regularly break into chemist shops and steal their drugs. Any drugs that were worth stealing were kept in special strongboxes with DDA marked on the side. These initials stood for *Dangerous Drugs Act*. It was handy having all the decent *gear* labeled in one box like this, because it saved us raking around in the aspirins. Most of the inner-city chemists were fitted with alarm bells, so we tended to stick to the provincial chemist shops where a decent jemmy and a pair of pliers would be all we needed for a successful raid.

It was around that time that I started experimenting with drugs. AIDS hadn't been heard of yet and it was considered quite a manly Scottish thing to do to stick a needle in your arm. Much the same as drinking ten pints of lager and then eating a spicy curry. The climate in Dundee is generally quite cold but it was common for 'would be' *hard men* to parade around in singlets to show off their bandages and track marks. Anybody that had already contracted Hepatitis was considered *really hard*. Yes, those were the *golden years*, when if you didn't use your arm as a pin-cushion, you were obviously a metrosexual fucking sodomite. There would be queues of blokes in pub toilets waiting to share some dirty old horse spike. Whoever was using the needle would suck the water into the syringe straight from the toilet bowl because this water was 'distilled'. Fuck knows how that myth came about, but it was definitely considered to be the hygienic way to bang up. Guys would be crushing up whatever pills they could get their hands on and

31

trying them out in their veins. It was often pot-luck and sometimes they would get a buzz on, but a lot of times they would be disappointed with the effect. If some bloke collapsed mid fix, the next guy in line would just fish the spike out of his arm and carry on. Vodka was apparently gentler on the veins but had less *oomph* than some of your more rumbustious malts.

One evening after a successful raid on a chemist in Forfar, the gang and I headed back to a safe-house with the booty. The mood was quite festive and corks were popping all around. Corks from medicine bottles! Big Ogie was filling his syringe with pharmaceutical *heroin* when I caught his eye.

"C'mere you yi wee fuckin poof," demanded the man-mountain, as he got me in a headlock and maximized his physical intimidation prerogative.

I meekly rolled my sleeve up and the big man administered my first ever hit of *smack*. I didn't really fancy a needle in the arm, but I didn't fancy 'BO' carved into my face either, so I went quietly. I lay on the floor in a dream-like state for the next four hours. The *Lucky For Some* gang were my favourite people in the world and big Ogie was next to God. All my troubles faded as I lay cocooned in an ecstatic back-in-the-womb-like stupor.

I began punting *gear* for the gang and got a few customers of my own. I had several casual users, but my main *heroin* customers were a charming couple of scallywags who would ring me at all hours and ask me to bring them *gear*. Their names were Nipper Andersen and Heather McLeish. It was a kind of love-hate relationship between Heather and Nipper. He loved her but she seemed to fucking hate him. She still had beautiful eyes and long dark hair, but her arse and tits had all but disappeared. It seemed as though the pills, booze, *smack* and prison sentences had all taken their toll, and years of battling against herself had left her stern-faced and bitter.

Nipper always had a fag end hanging out of his mouth. Nipper is Dundonese for fag end, hence the nickname. He was completely over the hill at just forty years of age. His hair had tumbled from his head as had the teeth from his mouth. Years of jagging himself with dirty needles had rendered him the carrier of every disease under the sun. AIDS hadn't been invented then, but there was a whole host of other intravenous diseases to choose from. Although Nipper wasn't much good at anything, there was one function that he could do quite proficiently, and that was acting as a decoy or a stooge. As soon as he went in a store, alarm bells would sound in the store detectives' heads and they would buzz around him like bluebottles around shit. With his tattooed neck, shiny bald head, massive earrings and toothless grin, he was definitely one to be watched closely. As Nipper, the professional decoy, pranced through the stores like the *Pied Piper of Hamlet*, the bold Heather would spring into action. Being deft of hand and fleet of foot she would fill her roomy bags with all manner of goodies, then disappear into the crowded street before the stores knew what had hit them.

They were an industrious couple, but somehow their money was never enough to feed their considerable drug habits. Junk was their favourite tipple but anything else that happened to be on hand would be crushed up, put on a spoon and sucked up through the needle. I often watched Nipper bang up whiskey; he would fish around in his almost empty whiskey glass with his dirty old spike, suck it into the syringe and then mainline it! The masochistic bastard would then roll around on the floor in agony, screaming that his veins were on fire, only to be followed five minutes later by a repeat performance of the process by injecting in the other arm.

33

Professional decoys were ten a penny in Dundee. The pubs were full of unemployed, dodgy looking bastards who could fill Nipper's shoes tomorrow, and Heather wasted no time in reminding him of this. Basically Heather wore the *troozirs,* so whenever drugs were procured, Nipper would always allow Heather to have first use of the needle. However there was one problem with this order of play. That was due to the fact she had been using her body as a pin cushion for so many years she hardly had any veins left, so it took her forever to take a hit. Nipper would moan like fuck for her to hurry up and find a vein so that he could have a jab; begging, pleading and rolling on the floor to no avail. Heather was fixing up first and that was the end of it, even if it took her all day to find a vein. This was a real bone of contention between them and Nipper would curse her blind every day. Unfortunately for him there wasn't much he could do about it.

As usual, it was Heather that rang me very early one morning asking me to bring her some *smack.* I told her to expect me in an hour. Unfortunately I had to see a man about a dog and showed up at her door not one hour but two hours later. I arrived to find the front door wide open. Hesitating, I wondered whether I should high tail it out of there, as there was a high possibility that the filth may be hanging about. It was completely out of character for Nipper and Heather to leave their front door wide open. Nipper's dog, a sad three-legged mongrel aptly named Skippy, was now standing in front of me. Perhaps I had watched too many Lassie movies as a kid, but I swear this dog was conveying some kind of distress signal to me by it's whimpering. So taking the bull by the horns and following the dog, I ventured slowly inside. Rasping noises could be heard coming from the front room and I surmised that either Nipper was giving Heather a portion, or he was having a severe asthma attack. Opening the door where the sound was coming from, I stopped in shock as I took in the sight that met my eyes. Nipper was dangling from the rafters, a leather belt around his neck, a wooden chair fallen sideways onto the floor. The silly bastard had tried to hang himself. It seemed like an eternity, but must have only been a matter of seconds, before I sprang in to action. I ran into the kitchen to get a knife to cut him down. Holding his body as best I could I cut through the belt. It was hard going but eventually the knife won. Taking his weight as his body was freed, I quickly laid him on the ground and started to pump his chest with my hands. Cardiac arrests are quite common among *junkies* so I knew what to do. Poor old Nipper's face was a deathly blue and his lips were purple and swollen, but after several minutes pumping he began to breathe and in unison with Nipper, I breathed too. Yet mine was a sigh of relief, as I don't think I could have ever brought myself to give him the kiss of life!

"Ah wisnae trying tae top masel, man, it wiz an accident," croaked Nipper

"Funny fuckin' accident, Nipper! Are you trying tae tell me you accidentally stood on a chair tied a belt round yir neck and accidentally kicked away the chair?"

"I wiz jist trying tae generate a bit ae sympathy."

"Bit fuckin extreme Nipper is it no? If ah hudnae ah come up them stairs mate you'de be broon fucking bread! Fat lotta fuckin' good sympathy widda done yi then."

"Ah wisnae looking fir sympathy fae you. Ah wiz looking fir sympathy fae her."

"Who the fuck is her? There's naebody here except you me and that mangy mutt!"

"Exactly, mangy mutt indeed. Heather had gone off tae score cause we got fed up waiting for you tae show up. You ken how lang it always takes her tae fix up, and I am sick and tired o' having tae squirm and shake till that ball breaking bitch has a hit, so I decided to go for the sympathy angle. Ah'v left the front door off the latch and arranged tae jump aff the chair when ah heard her come through the front door. As soon as ah heard a noise ah kicked away the chair and guess who opened the door? Fucking Skippy!"

9

UP YIR KILT

NOW THAT I was earning a crust from my illegal activities, I decided to pursue the activity that I had missed most during my unlawful incarceration. Sexual habits differ from culture to culture and perhaps the Scottish mating game needs further explanation. Scottish women in general seem to be receptive to the caveman approach. The male members of this macho society (where men are men and sheep wear wellies) truly appreciate beauty. In fact we even have a special name for beautiful women in Scotland. We call them tourists! Although there is no official border between Scotland and England, you can always tell when you've entered the historical land of the Picts because the cows are far better looking than the women. Scotland's unofficial national anthem is actually 'Hey MacLoud! Get off of my ewe.' In fact the new Scottish Barbie Doll comes with twelve kids, a dole check and a drinking problem.

If you ever needed concrete proof of Darwin's 'survival of the fattest' theory, then look no further than the Scottish mating game, played out every Saturday in pubs and clubs, bars and discos, chip shops and bingo halls. On this holiest of holy days, the nation is absorbed by that opiate of the masses - football. Though the womenfolk are not directly involved in the conversations surrounding this pastime, their active cooperation is nevertheless essential to the smooth running of the day's events.

Saturday would typically start with the female members of the household rising bright and early to attend to domestic chores. The traditional tribal costume men wear for these occasions will be dusted, pressed, and in general made ready. The tribal costume is however not compulsory, as some men prefer to affect no decoration whatsoever. This allows them more freedom of movement behind enemy lines. The readying of the costume will differ from household to household, and the choice of how to present himself at the match is entirely at the discretion of the male. This, of course, can be a cause of great confusion among the gentler sex, who through no fault of their own, cannot be expected to comprehend the intricate delicacies of a man's sartorial approach to match day. An ill-chosen scarf may, for instance, inspire great hostility from an opposing tribe, and could result in the most unfortunate circumstance of preventing our protagonist from arriving home by his preferred mode of transport, which more often than not would be train or omnibus, and not by the means described in the threatening diatribe of a losing side, "YOU'RE GOING HOME IN A FUCKING AMBULANCE!"

Next, the breakfast (a heart attack on a plate) is made ready. This normally consists of lardy sausages, lardy eggs, lardy chips and some more lard just for good measure. Only now, the male Homo Sapien is gently prodded from his quiet dreams of nutmegs and injury time clinchers. He makes his way belching and farting towards the thunder box for his morning ablutions. The shaving ritual may include the cranium, depending on the level of fierceness this particular specimen wishes to portray. Skinheads tend to look hard even if they're as soft as shite! After being watered and fed and his costume donned, the male is almost ready for the off.

Raking through his toolbox of knuckledusters, chibs and flickies, Fatboy will choose his weapon. Again the poor women folk, dreadfully undermined in this phallocentric hetero-patriarchalist society, are at a loss in this matter and are often heard asking the daftest of questions.

"Will ah get yir wee flick knife oot the cupboard for ye, Wullie?"

"For Christ's sake wumman! It's the Rangers we're playing t'day, no' the bloody boy scouts. Now bring me the hatchet! The green and white one wi' the Pope's face painted on the handle."

Sandwiches and Bovril flask in hand, Fatboy sallies forth whistling some catchy sectarian ditty, the lyrics of which will pertain to either some Knoxian notion of a hand-me-down sash for the doubters of papal inflammability (light a match and see!), or a merry ploughboy who leaves behind a girl called Mary for the left-footers.

Now that the women have been left to their own devices, they begin to plan the days activities. Most of these will centre on beautifying themselves for the evening's festivities, when the men folk return home from the day's sporting event and the real games begin.

As we have already ascertained, Scottish women tend to disappoint in the looks department as gravity takes its heavy toll. It is a well-known fact that most married women in Scotland are in fact so rough that the majority of husbands would rather take their wives to work rather than have to kiss them goodbye in the morning.

There are a number of contributing factors to the dire state of the Scottish women-folk, the most obvious being bad diet, harsh climate and lack of funds. Beauticians were thin on the ground in bonny Scotland because the sheer immensity of the task at hand would snap the purse strings off your average Scottish wifie. She would be more likely get an estimate from a beautician than a price. Nevertheless, these brave females, against all odds, would launch themselves headlong into the hoary task. All day until early evening the women-folk will primp and pose, pluck the nose, lash and lush, pluck and brush, crimp and curl, knots unfurl, paint the toes, powder the nose. Doused with hair spray and perfume these feisty females footer forwards in fuck-me footwear for a fun filled evening.

If the male's team is playing at home, it would be customary to nip home for a shit, shower and shave before going out on the pull. If, on the other hand, it were an away game, there wouldn't be time for this, so he would more than likely go straight out dressed in full tribal costume, fanning the flames of sectarian strife. This could result in the unfortunate likelihood of having your legs broken rather than the original plan, which was to get your leg over, sing a sectarian song and end up in theatre.

The intermingling of the sexes doesn't really begin until later-on in the disco, so during the early stages of the evening in the pub, the genders remain split. Small clusters of men gather together and noisily reminisce about missed sitters, four-eyed referees and biased officials. The women-folk will discreetly place themselves within spitting distance of whatever male they fancy, and bat their eyelids patiently 'til Don Juan is pissed enough to give some sign indicating that he might be interested in getting together later. This confirmation of interest would normally be a wink or a half-smile, but in the case of a real smoothie the interest might even stretch to a verbal forray.

"Ur yi goin tae the disco later, Morag? Aye? Well I might see ye in there."

To the untrained ear this might sound like an offhand remark, but in making the statement, Romeo has now thrown his cards on the table. He's let it be known to Morag that if she plays her cards right, she might end up as this evening's object of desire. It is a brave move on his part. These kind of words words must be uttered well out of the earshot of his mates, as Scottish men are not really big on cutting the carpet and usually leave the dancin' tae the lassies, while they prop up the bar trying tae look hard.

As the evening comes to a close at the disco, the DJ will traditionally play a few slow songs to indicate that it'll soon be chucking oot time. At this signal, the plucky males will dash to the dance floor and tap a lassie on the shoulder and utter the famous words.

"Are ye dancin'?"

Having ensconced the chosen female in a beery hug, Romeo will then enquire with uniform unoriginality, "Can I take you up the road?"

This seemingly innocent question is actually a request for sex, and Dundee women are fully aware that an affirmative answer to this question is an invitation to amorous advances. It may not be an open invitation for full penetrative sex but it has to at least include the promise of a cup of tea and a carry-on. As the eager young couples hurry homewards through the dark and frosty night, and the city rests in quiet slumber, one cannot help but speculate that if there is a God in heaven, He can now sit back and relax in the comforting knowledge that the proliferation of the species is assured.

10

THOU SHALT NOT KILL

MY FATHER SEEMED to continuously lament the fact that I couldn't be like everyone else and get a proper job. My older brother Tony worked on the oil rigs, which did pay well, but it meant freezing your bollocks off in the North Sea for months at a time with nothing to look at except the fat hairy roustabouts. I'd already had just about all I could take of all male environments in Borstal.

My little brother Danny had a job making golf clubs at the famous St Andrew's. He seemed very happy and well adjusted compared to big bad me. Danny married his childhood sweetheart Diane at sixteen. The daft little bastard had got her up the stick so he didn't have much choice but to tie the knot. I didn't envy him though; stinky nappies, shopping with the wife and all the other garbage that goes with settling down. Thanks, but no thanks.

The pharmaceutical trade in my immediate environs began to get a bit more competitive. There was a mob from Fife called The Chapter, a biker gang with nearly two thousand members. My crew was hard but we couldn't compete with their numbers or their armoury. There was a lot of fighting round the pubs and clubs, a few shootings and stabbings as these guys pretty much took over the town. They were always team-handed except for the occasional times when we would catch a couple of them dealing in a club on our patch, and by jings would we give them what for. The word was out on the street that The Chapter was now gunning for us!

Our gang was apparently on The Chapter's assassination list. This death list was the talk of the town, so I fancied grabbing some of the spotlight myself. One particular night, a Thursday, I was in a pub when I happened to spot Chopper Flynn at the bar. He was one of the top men in The Chapter and there he was having a bevy with a right tasty looking bit of fluff. He was a greasy, longhaired, fat, bearded biker bastard, and he was all over the tart like a rash; one hand down her knickers, the other one cupping her tit and his tongue half-way down her throat. God, I hate people carrying on like that in public. Why don't they go home and shag behind closed doors like decent folk? The bird wasn't daft though, because she had one hand on his knob while the other hand was fishing around in his jacket pocket. She definitely wasn't after him for his looks, the fat cunt.

Chopper didn't know my face from Adam but I recognised him immediately. Standing well out of his line of vision, I watched him like a hawk. After he had finished having a grope he wiped his mingeing hands on his filthy jeans. He was smoking joints, drinking whiskey chasers and looked well out of his box. I watched as the fat greasy bastard got up and staggered towards the bog. After waiting about thirty seconds, I followed him inside. He was standing with legs parted pissing into the urinal, one arm stretched out, hand against the wall. The other hand grasped a rather large willy (perhaps that's why they called him Chopper, and not as everyone presumed, because he used to hack people up). He was rather unsteadily waving it about trying to aim in the direction of the urinal, but not succeeding as the piss was going everywhere. Taking my position next to him I pretended to piss, while discreetly slipping the brass onto my knuckles.

"Scuse me mate. Do you know a guy called Dennis Sweeney?"

He turned his head and looked at me with bloodshot eyes.

"No. Why?"

"Well, you fucking do now!"

I smashed the duster right into his nose. Chopper staggered backwards holding his hands up to his ugly mug. His knob was still hanging out so I kicked the bastard in the bollocks. He screamed like a banshee! I gave him a high kick to the head and he fell to his knees roaring like a bull, so for good measure I put some well-placed kicks into his face and throat. Just getting into my stride now. Chopper was beginning to look like a fucking train wreck when who should walk in, catching me in the act, but the fucking slag that he had been sucking face with. She proceeded to scream the place down, at the same time as grabbing my hair and clawing at my face. Her fucking screaming was doing my nut in, so I lamped her one in the kisser. My handiwork lay covered in blood in front of me, Chopper was still spread-eagled across the floor, well fucked. The tart tried to help him get up.

"Sebastian. Oh my God! Sebastian, are you OK?"

I was pissing myself laughing as I fled the scene before plod showed up. Wait until the town gets to know that Chopper Flynn got a beating and his real name is Sebastian! Of course after that, it was the talk of the town that Sebastian Flynn was going to kill Dennis Sweeny. There's nothing like a price on your head to bring the birds flocking. I loved the attention. Mad, bad and dangerous to know! All I do is give...

There were a few close scrapes with The Chapter after the confrontation with Chopper and his girl, but I had the good sense to avoid their hangouts and they stayed well clear of ours. One night, after this incident had been pretty much put to the back of my mind, a weedy looking guy comes running into the pub, gasping for breath.

"Hey Den! Your brother's been stabbed!." I don't know how he knew my name because I had never seen the cunt before.

I ran like fuck down the street and saw an ambulance outside a pub. The police had cordoned off the front door of the place and were questioning people about the incident. Pushing my way through the onlookers, I told the coppers that the bloke that had been stabbed was my brother, so they allowed me into the pub. Danny was sitting on a bench surrounded by flatfoots. What had once been a good-looking face was now covered in hundreds of small cuts. Some bastard had stuck a broken glass in his face. Even though Danny was in a terrible state and needed hospital treatment, the coppers wouldn't let him go, instead insisting on firing questions at him. With pencils in hand, they busily scribbled their questions and Danny's answers into their pathetic little notebooks.

"How do you know they were gang members?"

"Did you do something to annoy them?"

There was blood seeping through the side of Danny's jumper and oozing between the fingers of his hand as he tried to ease the pain, his face wincing in the process.

"Just get him in the ambulance! What's wrong with you? You and you're fucking questions!" I shouted, pushing my way between the coppers until I reached Danny. He was now as white as a ghost and these idiots were wanting to know his date of birth. A big fat slag of a policewoman poked her stick towards my face and shouted.

"Just you calm down now, Sonny."

"Just get him to a doctor for fuck's sake!"

45

The fat cow kicked me in the shins so I threw her stick on the ground, which caused six coppers to start laying into me just as Danny was being helped out the door. Even in his weakened state Danny tried to stop them hitting me, but to no avail. I was nicked and taken to the cop shop, given another beating, and thrown in the stinking cells. I felt so hopeless. I didn't know if someone had mistaken Danny for me, or maybe they knew he was my brother and just did him anyway. Drunks were singing and fighting in the other cells, and every now and then the coppers would come down team-handed and give someone a kicking. The thuds of hobnailed boots contacting flesh made me feel sick to my stomach. This violent lifestyle had once seemed glamorous to me, but now? And what about wee Danny? The poor bastard wouldn't hurt a fly, yet now he was lying in the hospital with stab wounds and a face physically scarred for life. I could almost hear my father's voice. "You no good waster, now look what you've gone and done!." Of course he was right, it was all my fault. I was entirely to blame, being a no good, malicious thug. This was my payback time, only instead of knifing me they took their revenge out on Danny. I knocked on the cell door and called out.

"Turnkey. Turnkey."

The guys who lock you in the cells aren't real coppers, so they sometimes have an ounce of humanity left in them.

"Scuse me. Turnkey." The turnkey came up and opened the small hatch.

"What is it?"

"Would ye do is a favour? Would ye phone up the emergency department at the hospital and see if ma wee brither's okay? He's been stabbed. I jist want tae know if he's OK. Would yi dae that fir is, turnkey? He's only a bairn."

"Ah'll find oot fir ye. Jist hang on, son."

The turnkey locked the hatch and walked away. I sat on the cell floor licking my wounds. The police had certainly earned this week's pay packet; my ankle had swollen up like a balloon and my head was cut in several places too. After about half an hour I heard the turnkey's footsteps coming toward my cell. He unlocked the hatch.

"Ah'm afraid I have some bad news for yi son. Yir brither passed away. Complications from the knife wound." I sat down on the bed and held my head between my hands.

"Will ye be all right, son?"

"Aye, don't worry."

"Ahm awfy sorry."

"No as sorry as am gonnae be."

He locked the hatch and walked away leaving me alone to face my misery. Danny dead, me to blame. That was the fight knocked out of me there and then. Sure I could hunt down whoever killed him and avenge my brother's death, but to what end? It wouldn't bring him back, just more misery heaped upon my long-suffering family. No, I wasn't going to kill anyone; I was going to get my sorry arse out of Scotland forever and ever. Amen!

11

LONDON'S CALLING

MY FATHER BAILED me out of jail and drove me back home. The rain battered off the car as we drove through the narrow grey streets. I wasn't really listening but he went on and on about what a waste of space I was. Never darken his doorstep again was the gist of it, and to be honest I had to agree with him. What else could he do? He was after all the man of the house and had to look at things on a larger scale. There were other more deserving members of his brood that needed protecting. I know it broke his heart to give me the bums rush but a man's got to do what a man's got to do. 'If thy right hand offendeth thee, cut it off!' Just like the good book says.

When I arrived home I packed some clothes into my boxing kitbag, then I left for Tay Bridge train station without even talking to my parents. My mother was crying in the kitchen. I couldn't even look at her I felt so ashamed, so I left as quietly as I could out the front door. I had the address of some Dundee guys who were living in a squat at the Elephant and Castle in South East London, so I headed on down to the big smoke. The guys didn't look too happy initially; nothing personal, it just meant less floor space all round. The morning after I arrived, I went along with one of the blokes from the squat to the building site where he worked, and got a start as a hod-carrier. It was hard graft but at least it kept my mind off how much of a fuck-up I was. It was OK for a few weeks. Smoking spliff all day at work and getting drunk at night took my mind off my brother's death, but after a while it started to become a bit tedious. We could all play Jack the lad in Scotland, but our inability to mingle with the natives down here was becoming painfully obvious. London was really bringing it home to me how socially ill-equipped me and the lads in the squat really were. If the good old British class system were divided into a scale of one to ten, the Scots would score a big fat zero. To save ourselves the embarrassment of not being understood, we tended to converse mainly with other members of our race. Chained by our linguistic fetters we would only venture forth from our local pub to meet other vocal McCripples in their sad little pubs, there to wistfully lament about the good old days 'up the road'.

It wasn't as if we were hostile or unfriendly. We were, in point of fact, painfully shy. On the odd occasion some girl would make the brave attempt to join our company, we would all clam up like schoolboys, nodding and smiling but saying very little. It vexed me greatly to watch the flash little Cockney wankers charming the knickers off all the women. Anytime I tried to come across as a silver-tongued scallywag it sounded as if I was clearing my throat. I tried my damndest to sound windswept and exotic but it would come out all wrong. My pathetic attempts at conversation were muddled in some unintelligible Scottish burr. I would hasten back to my clansmen with my tail between my legs, where we would then engross ourselves in the macho pursuits of pool or darts whilst the world passed us by.

Something had to be done! Action had to be taken. How was I to bridge the great divide? Elocution lessons? Anger management? Enrol in a Swiss finishing school? No, there was no alternative in my mind but to temporarily turn my back on my roots. Otherwise, there was no way I was going to get a leg over. I would have to go on a recce mission into the enemy camp; a simian Eliza Doolittle.

I went straight to the heart of the matter and joined a South London boxing club. They might take the piss out of my countrified speech in the pub, but just let the smug little bastards try it in the ring. I felt at home as soon as I walked through the boxing club door, dragging my knuckles behind me. 'Take me to your leader.'

The familiar noises and smells, the flat noses and greasy, spotty youths prancing around in vests in front of mirrors emitting the familiar "Mhew Mhew, Mhew" from their nasal cavities, was all very familiar to me now. Although the Scottish accent sounded out of place amongst the Cockneys, when it came to throwing punches we all spoke the same lingo. The trainer was a tough looking bloke in his mid forties; he was doing some pad work in the ring with some of the boys. His nose, like that of most old boxers, was so flat it was almost flush with his face.

"Excuse me mister... Do ya mind if I join the club?"

"What's that Jock? Can't understand ya. Wot did you say?"

One of my pet hates was being referred to as Jock. It's a term that in my opinion should only be used light-heartedly amongst friends, and in very few situations. There were a lot of black fellas calling each other niggers, and that's OK amongst themselves, but for this knees up muvva brown barra boy to give it the big one on our first meeting was completely unnecessary in my opinion.

"I would like to join this club, if that is OK with you." My tone of voice indicated that I wasn't in the mood for any Scottish jokes.

"Awright Jock. Come up Friday seven o'clock. Done a bit 'ave ya?"

"Yes. A bit."

Walking out onto the street of darkest Bermondsey, I uncharacteristically felt some empathy for the Cockneys. It wasn't a great start in life to be born in one of these sprawling concrete jungle council estates, the majority of which sported boarded up windows. Graffiti was sprayed on every reachable area of the walls. Cat killers, pyromaniacs, rapists, wife beaters, alcoholics, refugees and war babies from all over the world; escaping oppression from foreign military regimes and ending up in a tower block in no-man's land, with it looking more like a war zone than the shitey hole they just escaped from. Dole checks, vandalism, muggings, theft and other such socio-economic strife. Welcome to the 'Land of Hope and Glory'. Not that Scotland was any better by comparison. The only advantage of being Scottish in London was that the police couldn't tell I was black 'til I opened my mouth.

The next Friday, as soon as work had finished for the day, I went straight down to the boxing club to join up. I went into changing room and got my gear on, then started warming up by shadow boxing in front of the mirror. The trainer showed up shortly afterwards and got the boxers organized for a training session. There were about twenty guys training, and by the way they were pounding the bags, some of them looked pretty handy. Most of them were lightweights, a few looked nearer my weight, welter, and just one guy was a middleweight. Me and the other boxers trained for about an hour, then everybody started getting gloved up to do some sparring. The boys were putting on their bandages and putting in their gum shields, while I just carried on shadow boxing. After a few of them had sparred, the trainer turns round to me.

"Oi Jock! Do you wanna move arahnd a bit?"

"My name isn't Jock!"

"Don't get the 'ump Jock, we're only 'aving a giraffe."

It was stupid of me to show that being called Jock annoyed me, but it was a weird expression he had used for sparring. He had indicated it was going to be a light spar by asking me, if I wanted "to move around a bit."

My father used to train the Scottish national team. Anytime things got out of hand during a spar, my father would stop the boxers and tell them that if they wanted to get heavy they should save it for a contest. It made sense to keep things pretty light during sparring sessions; it was the only way to learn. Boxers don't mind trying out new combinations or moves if you know that someone isn't going to take your head off when you make a mistake or drop your guard. A fight is a fight, a contest is a contest, but sparring is different. In a fight or a contest, if your opponent sees a chance he will hurt you, but sparring is more like theory and you have to know it is safe to make a mistake.

The middleweight got gloved up and climbed in the ring. There was steam rising from him after building up a sweat on the heavy bag. He had a thick bull-like neck and an unfortunate spiky hairstyle that looked like it had been cut by the council. The trainer told me to get myself in the ring, and before I had time to prepare myself he rang the bell. The middleweight came at me flat-footed with both hands. His punches were more powerful than mine, but I was faster. Jab and move. Jab and move. He was getting frustrated with my tactics and came at me harder, trying to pin me on the ropes. His mates, the other boxers and even the trainer began cheering him on. I felt like I was surrounded by a pack of wild dogs. It was bad enough trying to stay out of raging bull's way without these wankers putting in their two bobs worth.

"Give it to the Jock bastard! Fucking haggis cunt!"

I managed to stay out of trouble for most of the first round, clinging to the belief that this was only a spar and eventually things would calm down. When the bell went for the break however, just by the way the guys were egging him on, it was obvious that things were going to get out of hand. There was not one person in the club that hadn't gathered around the ring, and there were nods and winks from all sides. The bell went again and the next round began, the bastard coming at me with both fists flying.

"Give it to him! C'mon get the Jock bastard!"

He was very powerful and he started catching me with a few. I was trying desperately to stay out of his way but there's nowhere to hide in a boxing ring. This was no longer a spar; the cunt had backed me into the corner. I tried to fake a body swerve to get out but he had me hemmed in, letting fly with both his fists. Even though I tried to weave and parry, he was coming on far too strong. He left me with no choice. I hit him with a left hand that was so powerful it nearly took his fucking head off. The bone in his nose made a horrible snapping sound as he slumped and fell, hitting the canvas like a sack of shit. Before I knew it a hoard of shocked Cock Sparrers invaded the ring in an attempt to revive him.

"You fucking Jock wanker! It's meant to be a spar!"

"It wasn't a spar a minute a go."

The trainer could have stopped it before it got nasty, but he obviously thought the middleweight was going to give Jock McScott a doin'. Different fucking story now!

12

HONEY BOY LLOYD AND I-SELF

AFTER THE EPISODE with the middleweight, remarkably, I was still allowed to continue training at the club. But lessons were not learnt, as the sparring sessions were always the same; no leeway. Guard up, fists clenched, one mistake and you were punished for it. These sparring match-ups proved to be completely useless as training sessions, because nobody learned anything new. There was only one bloke really I enjoyed sparring with, definitely a cut above the rest. He was polite, helpful, friendly, and never referred to me as Jock. And when we sparred together, we really did spar. There was an unspoken understanding between us that we wouldn't take each other's heads off for making a mistake. It was very satisfying being able to improve my speed, agility and punching combinations, knowing that I was with a sparring partner who didn't want to kill me. His name was Lloyd Honeygan and he was the wrong colour for a South London Cockney boxing club. The members all made it quite clear that they didn't like him, although no one would ever dare say anything to his face. Although it was obvious he wasn't welcome at this boxing club, he had the last laugh as he went on to become the world professional welterweight champion. He took the title from Don 'The Cobra' Curry, who some people rated as the best pound-for-pound fighter of his time.

Honeygan's talent was obvious even back then, as an amateur, but the trainers andother boxers couldn't see past his skin colour. He would jog to the club in his tracksuit, do his training, and leave again without talking to anyone, and without any one person even acknowledging his presence. With the exception of course on those days when sparring, whence the bold *Honey Boy* would administer unto his fair skinned *Cockney* brethren some *righteous ras clot licks*.

The first time I saw Honeygan training I was in the corner punching the bag. These two black men in tracksuits came bowling through the doors, and the *Cockneys* all looked at each other rolling their eyes as if to say 'here he comes again, the stroppy, wanker.'

Honeygan was wearing a tracksuit in the colours of the Jamaican flag. His friend had a huge *ghetto blaster* on his shoulder which he put down in the corner of the club and switched on. The music was *ragamuffin dance hall reggae* and Honeygan went through his training schedule to the sound of the *reggae* music blasting out. Most white boxers train as if they have a stick up their arse, and would look on in amusement at Honeygan while he displayed the qualities that they lacked. A lot of his bends and stretches were almost *ballet*. Most boxers are so caught up in an egotistical, tough guy illusion that it makes their mindset, exercises, training and sparring very stiff; and of course what they considered very '*man-like*'. Honeygan, on the other hand, was graceful. He flowed. The confidence oozed from him, not having any hang-ups about trying to look *hard*. He just was *hard*, no question about it.

My technique improved a whole lot, watching and training with this lean mean fighting machine. It wasn't about being *hard*. It was about speed, agility, flexibility, and scoring points; moving, dancing and outthinking your opponent. Sometimes whilst sparring with him he would take me to a level of competition that I didn't even know existed.

13

COCKNEY WANKERS

THE TRAINER AT the club got me a medical card and said he was going to fix me up with a contest. I hadn't really planned on fighting, I just wanted to train to keep my body and mind in condition.

Boxing clubs are always the same; people were not expected to just come and train. Like it or not, eventually you have to get with the programme. I therefore found myself in the position of being put on the Saturday billing for the following weekend of a club show at the *Savoy Hotel*. My refusal would have meant dropping out of the club, and as I didn't want to do that, I resigned myself to the inevitable. I trained hard the weekend before and every evening leading up to the fight. I was also going running in the mornings with Honeygan, who, it turned out, lived only a couple of streets away from me at the *Elephant and Castle*. The night of the contest arrived all too soon. Arriving early I could see they were expecting a big crowd. The hall was packed with tables and chairs, and busy looking officials guarded every entrance to stop people getting in without tickets. It was a *black-tie* do, with people such as Charlie Magri, Dickie Davies and Henry Cooper coming along to watch. It was clearly a special occasion for there was also a group of boxers from the famous Lambeth club

Fitzroy Lodge, who proudly wore their club's name emblazoned on their tracksuits.

My trainer pointed out my opponent, who was a stocky skinhead, a bit puffy round the eyes, looking like he had taken a bit of punishment in his time. Although a formidable looking opponent, he didn't appear to be very chronologically accomplished, so my ring-craft would come in handy. He was a couple of inches shorter than me but very wide, well formed, and more importantly looked like he could hit. We were billed to appear as the tenth contest.

A few of the younger boys fought first, and I helped the seconds in the corner, passing the water up for the kids to gurgle and spit between rounds. Our trainer knew his onions, as he had been a good pro in his day, and he was well respected in boxing circles. The advice he was giving the kids between rounds made sense. My personal opinion of him was that he was a *pie-and-mash eating, Chas and Dave* caricature, but that's not to say he wasn't a good trainer.

After a couple of fights, the trainer told me to go and get stripped in readiness for the fight. There was a crowd of maybe five hundred pissed-up geezers, and the aisles leading to the arena were heavy with cigar smoke. On the way back to the dressing room a table full of pissed-up toffs accosted me.

"I say young man. Are you fighting tonight?"

I told them I was and showed them my name on the programme. They eyed me up like I was a piece of meat ready for auction.

"He looks like a strong boy."

I hate people talking about me like I'm not there. The same dickhead piped up again.

"I'm afraid I have already bet my money on your opponent."

"Well, you've lost your money then."

They loved that. *Fighting Talk!* These were wankers who had probably never been in a fight in their lives, running to the *karzee* to whack themselves off at the thrill of seeing young boys punching the shit out of each other. Hungry slum-dwellers battering each other into submission to satisfy the selfish interests of the ruling class.

One of the other boxers helped me tie my bandages.

"Where's your gum shield *Jock*?"

"I don't wear gum shields. They clog up your breathing. Bad enough trying to catch your breath without a big lump of plastic stuck in your mouth!"

I was nearly ready to get going, my boxing boots and jock strap on, whilst my opponent, at the other end of the dressing room, didn't seem to be in much of a hurry. He had his shirt off and was warming up, so I watched his style. He was *orthodox*, which was good for me, as I'm a *southpaw* and it's usually easy to tie up the jab of an *orthodox* boxer. It's only when I meet other *southpaws* that my own awkwardness is turned against me.

He was a bruiser, a short muscular powerhouse. I figured that he would come at me with all he had. Short guys have to fight close, otherwise they will lose on points to a taller, more scientific boxer. So I would stay away from him at first, keeping him on the end of my jab, then I would be able to pick him off and wear him down. I would start moving forward throwing big lefts. In the third, I would pound the monkey cunt with both hands. I didn't want him to catch me looking at him, otherwise he might think he had me worried and I didn't want that.

I had butterflies in my stomach and the adrenalin was starting to pump. I began to throw a few shapes, but I didn't want to give too much away so I faked being orthodox. I was throwing jabs with my left hand and pretending my right was the big one. The bastard was paying no heed to my show of bravado whatsoever, and it was freaking me out of a bit. I understood only too well the psychological warfare that goes on before a fight, being in the game long enough to know that the real champions never show emotion.

I much prefer an opponent who gives me *the eye* before a fight. By trying to look *hard* they are actually showing their fear. If they were confident enough in their abilities, they wouldn't have to try to scare their opponent before the fight. Usually if my opponent really gives me *the stare* before a fight, I pretend to be scared, and avoid his gaze right up 'til the bell goes. Then you have the impact of shock as your opponent realizes it was a sham, and you go straight at him and let him have it right on the button. I kept trying to catch my opponent looking at me but he was totally nonchalant. Not a good sign.

There was a big black guy in the dressing room getting stripped for a fight, and I thought 'Thank fuck its not him I'm fighting.' He must have been six two and at least a *light-heavy*. I went out into the arena to get gloved up. One of the trainers tied the laces whilst the other massaged my neck and shoulders. Vaseline was rubbed on my face to stop the bleeding in case I got cut.

"Where's your gum shield *Jock*?"

"Don't need one."

"You fink you're a big man don't you *Jock*?"

"Big enough."

"By the way *Jock*, I forgot to tell you."

"Tell me what?"

"We changed your opponent," pointing to the big black guy.

"Why didn't you tell me?"

"I knew you woz a bottle job you fucking *Jock*. You ain't man enough to fight for our club anyway. Go on, fuck off 'ome then you *Jock* cunt!"

I was seething with anger. I wanted to pound the podgy little fucker's face there and then, but that would have to wait.

"I didn't say I wouldn't fight him. I'll have him, but you're next you mouthy little shite!"

"C'mon then *Jock*, 'ave a fucking go." The other trainer and some of his mates had to pull us apart. The crowd saw this and cheered for more.

"I'm gonna punch your lights out you fucking *Cockney* wanker!"

"Any time *Jock!* Any fucking time you like."

The previous contest had finished and it was time to walk to the ring. On the way, the trainer and I hurled heated insults at each other. Even after I had climbed through the ropes and he was standing in my corner he kept at it.

"Fucking bottle job, *Jock* cunt."

So I pushed the flat nosed bastard right down the stairs. The crowd loved it. They went completely *chicken oriental*. The referee waved me and the big man into the centre of the ring.

"Now you both know the rules. I want a clean contest. No hitting below the belt. When I say 'break', you break, and when I say 'box', you box. Shake hands now and when the bell rings, come out fighting."

As we shook hands I looked up at the guy. He had a huge height and weight advantage. I had been done up like a kipper.

The bell rang and we came at each other in the centre of the ring. The big guy threw three left-handed jabs at my face. I rolled with the punches but they were weak as piss anyway. Anybody who threw jabs like that didn't deserve to be in the ring. He couldn't even do the *nose-noise* properly. He was blowing air out of his mouth and making a grunting noise; obviously an absolute beginner. I moved inside, faked with a right, and came over the top with a huge left-handed haymaker that hit him flush on the face. One punch and it was over; curtains for the novice. The crowd went loopy and my trainer jumped in the ring and put his arm round me.

"See *Jock*, no problem! I told you it would be all right!"

Tosser! He was supposed to be on my side, so why wind me up me like that just before I got in the ring? Some people seem to think he was doing me a favour by getting me angry before the fight, but there is no room for anger in the boxing ring. He wasn't doing me any favours, instead he was trying to stitch me up, thinking my bottle would crash; the light-ale drinking, jellied-eel eating, Farah wearing, gold-chained Del-Boy wannabe. Fuck him and the Pearly King, rag-and-bone donkey he rode in on. Hedge-hopping son of a pikey whore! Hope his rabbit dies and he can't sell the hutch.

14

INGLAN' IS A BITCH

AFTER THE FIGHT, I walked past Piccadilly Circus and waited at the bus stop at the bottom of Regent Street to catch the number 53 back to my flat in the Elephant and Castle. It was pissing down with rain and the trophy I had just won was too big to go in my kitbag, so I tried to keep it under my jacket to stop it getting wet. The bus came and I jumped on. The conductor clocked the trophy and put his hands up in a boxing pose.

"Been fighting son?"

"Yup."

"D'ya win son?"

"Yeah."

"Well done! Been at it long?"

"Too long mate, too long"

I looked at my reflection in the bus window and noticed bruising under my left eye. The guy must have caught me a couple of times before I done him. Didn't notice feeling anything at the time; must have been the adrenalin that helped stem the pain. *Had I been at it long?* It felt as though I had been at it forever; ducking and diving, bobbing and weaving, keeping my guard up and my chin tucked in. Facing life was like facing some relentless opponent in the ring. I could try every slick defensive move I knew but it wouldn't help. I was on a hiding to nothing.

The bus crawled slowly through the West End traffic. The crowds of Christmas shoppers scurried from shop to shop attempting to avoid the biting cold wind. Just another shitty day in paradise, huh! Another week till Christmas Day, followed by Boxing Day and New Years Day, then a whole new calendar year full of special days that come attached with the required sentiments; Match Day and Veterans Day, Gay Day, Birthday, Holiday, Happy Day and Sad Day. How about couldn't *give a fucking monkey's day!* Olympic Games, Cup Finals, World Cups, charity events like Feed the World, Pull Your Pudding, Save the Whale, Hug a Tree, Grab a Granny, Suck a Lemon... The list was endless.

There seemed to be huge gaping hole inside of me. I wanted some answers but didn't know where to look. Feeling like there was a worldwide conspiracy afoot to keep me in a state of utter confusion. Making me so anaesthetized that I had no choice but to give up and let the experts get on with it. What a wonderful thing democracy is. You can *say what you like* as long as you *do as you're told*. Get a job, get a wife. Pay your rent, pay your taxes. Get a bank account, get a mortgage, Have some kids and buy a car. Save up for a holiday, then save for Christmas Day, Match Day, Birthday, and Anniversary day. Remember, don't have a Sick Day or you won't git no Pay Day. It all seemed so superficial, so inadequate. Where did it all lead? Dying Day of course! Lying in some hospital bed in 30 years time dying of some *'disease of civilization'*, up to my neck in debt, alcoholism, depression, loneliness, and insanity. There had to be more to life than this.

The bus arrived at the *Elephant and Castle* shopping centre where I got off and walked up Newington Butts to the *Pullens Estate*. The squat was empty when I got there; the lads would more than likely be playing darts in the local pub. As usual, they'd be standing segregated from the rest of the English speaking world, in a little area they had claimed for themselves and had aptly named *Scots' Corner.* The squat was a fucking mess as usual. I fancied a cup of tea but we were out of sugar, so I went next door to borrow some from my neighbour. His name was Jack, and he had just come back from spending a year travelling around Asia. I was hoping to get a glimpse of his girlfriend who was almost too beautiful for words,. Cheekbones to die for and a really posh voice. Not that she ever spoke to the likes of us, she was out of our league. We just overheard her speaking to Jack on the stairs when she walked past, completely oblivious to us. She wasn't rude or anything, we were just insignificant and beneath her station. Her silences were deafening when she passed us on the stairs. We nicknamed her the *'Ice Maiden'*, and were all too terrified to try and strike up a conversation. Social snobbery has been elevated to an instinct in England, and we lowly *porridge-munchers* knew our grubby place.

Jack invited me in and told me to sit down on the couch. He disappeared into the kitchen and emerged a few moments later with a couple of glasses of wine and a huge *spliff* in his mouth. He retrieved some video copies of the old *Kung Fu* TV series and stuck one of them in the video player, setting it to play. Then he handed me the *spliff* and lounged back on the couch next to me.

"Have a go on that mate, it's *Charras* from Manali. What happened to your eye Den?"

"Boxing match."

"You fucking *Jocks* are all the same. Fight, fight, fight! Why don't you get a life man?"

"Look mate, either I go to training three nights a week or I sit in the pub every night, usually ending up in a fight anyway.''

"You're different from those other *Jocks*, Den. Why don't you do something different, like go to college? Or travel? You can't be a fucking labourer all your life."

"I nearly went to University but I ended up in *Borstal*."

"So you're gonna spend the rest of your life pissed off with society because things didn't go your way?"

"What the fuck is it to you if I do?"

"Don't get defensive Den. I'm only offering an opinion."

"Yeah, well if I want your fucking opinion I'll tell you, OK."

We turned our attention to the TV where six cowboys had surrounded Cain (*Grasshopper* as he was called by the *Buddhist* monks). They looked dangerous, but Cain was calmly telling them that he didn't want to fight. His impassive attitude is pissing the cowboys right off. Cain is not intimidated and remains serene, standing his ground. There's a flashback to the *Shaolin Temple*, where the *Master* is instructing *Grasshopper*, in stilted English, how to strike without emotion.

"*Grasshopper*, let go of confusion and knowing will arise. Let go of fear and calm will arise. You can beat a thousand of your enemies but you must first beat yourself. Anger is like picking up a burning stick and throwing it at someone. You must first burn your own hand. Let go of anger, *Grasshopper*."

The cowboys are continuing to taunt Cain, trying to get him to retaliate, but still he restrains himself.

"Please, I don't want any trouble. Just allow me to pass."

The cowboys are now well pissed-off and drunk, their intentions apparent on their faces. They want to hurt him, and hurt him bad. Hate for this man had taken hold of their senses. How dare he try to thwart their anger. Cain's prolonged composure and restraint has convinced them that he is a coward and a pushover. Still Cain does not succumb to their anger, his only actions being to stand completely still on one leg in the *Heron* stance. The cowboys are no longer putting up with this unusual display and Cain's lack of interest in them, so they attack. Within seconds, it is all over. Cain, now having no option but to defend himself, *chop sockeyes* his way through to the next episode.

Jack and I clapped loudly from our front row seat, the couch. The wine and the *spliff* were really kicking in. Jack shoved on another episode.

"That could be you Den. You could be Cain."

"How'd you mean?"

"Well you can fight like him right? And you want to break free from the shackles of your environment, right? So why don't you become like the wandering aesthetic monk, and go in search of *The Way?*"

"*The Way?*"

"*The Way.* The Tao. The rhythm of life. The circle of communication. The driving power in all nature. The ordering principle behind all life. *The way of the warrior!*"

"What the fuck are you on about Jack?"

"I'm talking about you Den and who you think you are. An angry young man with a chip on his shoulder. The *Borstal* boy, the big *hard* man that hates the world. Your name, your religion, your country, your language, your whole belief system is second hand; they were all given to you. These things were not your choice and they aren't you. It all came from somewhere else, not from inside you. This is your conditioning, separating you from who you really are. If you go through life in the 'hard done by' mode you will be closed to all the good stuff out there. Try and experience the harmony, man, the interrelatedness. Bond with people, bond with nature, and above all else, bond with yourself. The reason you are angry is because of the circumstances into which you were born. You didn't choose these circumstances, so don't allow these circumstances to determine the rest of your life. Everything is in a constant state of flux. Everything changes. Who are you really Den? Underneath this jaggy veneer, who are you once you peel off all these labels that society has pinned on you? All that shit that blocks the light of your natural wisdom. Play your part in the comedy Den, but stop identifying with the role."

"You're losing me here Jack."

"Exactly Den! Lose yourself! You have to understand *what you are not* in order to understand *what you are*. Not me, not mine. The death of your ego. Re-incarnate yourself, right now. Pack your bags, go to the station, and leave yourself behind. Change is natural, the way of the universe. It was the last thing the *Buddha* said on his deathbed. All compound things decay. Work out your own destiny with diligence. In other words, stop clinging to things that have no substance; be flexible and go with the flow. A plant that is soft and pliable will bend with the wind, but a plant that is stiff and brittle will break off and die."

"If the *Buddha* was so smart why was he so fat?"

"That's not the real *Buddha*. The fat *Buddha* represents *plenty*, and he doesn't arrive for another couple of thousand years. The real *Buddha* was skinny. Some teachings say that he ate and used nothing but hemp for the six years leading to his enlightenment."

"You sure he was enlightened? Maybe he was just *stoned* out of his nut. Confucius, he say: '*Man who smoke joint in toilet, high on pot,*' or, '*Man fiddling under wheelbarrow not always mechanic.*' You smoke too much, Jack!"

"I'm being serious here man. I'm talking about *liberation*, Den. Freedom from the bondage of self. Freedom from our blinkered, prejudiced, opinionated thoughts. *If*

*you always do what you've always done you'll always
get what you always got."*

"And how do I go about achieving this so called
freedom?"

"Well you can start by getting as far away as possible from those pathetic *Jock* wankers you hang about
with. Why don't you jump on a plane and go to Asia.
I'm going straight back there as soon as I finish this poxy
degree."

"What am I gonna do when I get there?"

"Blow that bridge when you come to it man. Go
to Hong Kong. I've seen return tickets for two hundred
notes. That's a week's money for you. What the fuck
have you got to lose?

The more *stoned* I got, the more abstract yet somehow meaningful it all became. We were one and the
same. I am he. He is me. That bald little Chinese monk
on TV was beckoning me to follow the path, the way of
the warrior, the way of the *Grasshopper*. The monk was
right, change was the natural way of the universe. Things
were not always as they appeared to be. Just like the
great bard said.

"Upon a hill there stood a coo, it must have moved
its no there noo!"

"Upon a hill there stood a coo, a bull my God!"

We talked, drank, smoked some more, and the more
out of it I got the better it sounded. Jack was right. Go
away and leave myself behind. What did I have to lose?
It was high time I cashed my chips in.

15

WILL IT AFFECT MY GIRO?

HAVING WITHDRAWN MY savings from the bank and cashing my final giro, I bade my fellow jockobites a fond adieu and booked a cheap flight to Hong Kong. As with most Scottish subsidy junkies I was terrified that leaving the UK would affect my broo money, but what will be, will be. As Confucius says: 'A journey of a thousand miles begins with the first step.'

Stansfield airport, named after the singer Lisa, is quite a distance from central London. I sat looking out the train window on the way to the airport pondering Jack's final words.

'Remember Den, no matter where you go, there you are, unless you leave yourself behind.'

Apparently he was referring to the death of my ego. I made a thorough search of all my belongings, even checking hemlines or stash pockets just in case I had hidden a bit of puff or some pills. And there was definitely no evidence of anything resembling an ego in any of my belongings. I had a kilt, some bagpipes, my *Dundee Football Club* shirt, a tin of *Fray Bentos* and a bottle of *Buckfast*, but couldn't really identify anything that resembled an ego.

I boarded the Hong Kong bound flight and was seated next to a youngish bloke who seemed to have put a lot of effort into trying to *dress down*. I wasn't sure what look it was he was trying to perfect, and clearly neither did he. I guessed he was one of those white middle class mummy's boys who thought they were *black*. He was wearing a baseball cap turned back-to-front. Actually it made him look more like a duck hunter than a home-boy. In a *Mockney* accent, he introduced himself as a student, which tempted me to introduce myself as hod carrier. He informed me that he had just finished his degree, and was having a year off before deciding which line of toil to pursue. It was the first time I had come across this 'year off' phenomena. What a fanciful notion it seemed to be. Most of my associates and community could hardly afford a day off in their miserable puffs without the *voracious hounds of debt* snapping hungrily at their heels. In their future, death would come as a welcome respite to their grey lives, as they sink dishonoured into the cosy oblivion of the grave...

Yet here was *Mr Student* having a whole year off!

With myself as a reluctant listener, he mused over the countries he would visit and the activities he might pursue. Mountain climbing in Nepal, surfing in Bali, even crocodile hunting in Australia. For all his *devil-may-care* nonchalant posturing, it was clear that mummy and daddy had furbished their little *precious* with every necessary comfort. He probably had return flight tickets, credit cards, emergency numbers, vaccinations, malaria shots, diarrhoea pills, water purifying tablets, a chest wig and maybe even a teddy bear for good measure. Oh, and of course he had the most comprehensive Hong Kong guidebook available. I must have overlooked the buying of such a book in my non-existent travel preparations. I tried to half-inch one at the airport but the hatchet-faced old bag behind the counter wouldn't take her eyes off me.

After a long and fairly uneventful trip, we prepared to land in Hong Kong. The airplane's descent path into

Hong Kong at that time went right between two huge apartment buildings, flying so close to them that I could actually see what the people inside were having for their tea. In fact, if the pilot had flown one ball-hair closer, our collective teas would have been on the table, pilot included.

On our way through customs, I had my first butchers of the Hong Kong *old bill*. My time served with the *Cockneys* was paying off, I knew all the jargon. Therefore, I brought *Mr Student's* attention to the strange apparel of the Hong Kong constabulary.

"Oi, geezer, 'ave a butcher's at the tin flute on that filf. 'ee must be 'avin a tin baff."

"Terribly sorry Scotchman old chap, but you really will have to speak slower. I am having tremendous difficulty adjusting my ears to your extremely coarse brogue."

"I said, yonder policeman chappies can't be serious in that get up, what, what."

The constable was wearing a khaki-coloured safari suit number with nifty little short pants, and a gun belt which looked completely out of place. As camp as a scoutmaster's sleeping bag with knee length white socks, which I bet he kept on whenever he indulged his penchant for porcine fudge-packery, splay-thighed and *sans culottes*.

Mr Student had a name, which he informed me was Farquar, and that he was actually Scottish too. I couldn't for the life of me work out which part of him was Scottish; perhaps a toe nail. We caught the underground to a station called Tsim Tcha Tsui. Here we re-surfaced on Nathan Road, one of Hong Kong's major shopping areas. It looked just like it did in the movies; markets, fruit sellers and flashing neon lights. There was a definite buzz about the place, with a vibrant *shop-'til-you-drop* kind of energy. Movers and shakers in a mad hurry to get wherever it was they were going. We found the address for a traveller's hostel listed in Farquar's book. It was situated on the sixteenth floor of a building called *Chun King Mansions*. After walking through a shopping arcade we found a lift and got on. Every time the lift stopped on the way up we were eyed suspiciously by the inhabitants of each floor. There were Indian curry houses, doss houses, brothels, *Karaoke* bars. Dodgy looking geezers of every size, shape and colour jumped on and off the lift as we rose higher; a labyrinthine monument to dodgy Asian goings-on.

Upon arriving at the sixteenth floor we were shown our bunk beds in dormitory-style rooms. The place was so dirty you had to wipe your feet on the way out. Even the mice were wearing overalls and driving round in dune buggies. Farquar found another bunch of 'year off' trust-afarians to hang out with, and they huddled together over bottles of water in the canteen. They pored over maps, trying to work out the cheapest, most uncomfortable routes to take from A to B. No doubt they planned to live on fish-heads and rice, and sleep toe to foot in fleapits across Asia. A few year's down the line, these well-shod sixth-form *lefties*, with silver shovels in their gobs, would metamorphose into *charlie*-sniffing, sex-pat corporadoes. They'd relinquish all pretences of honesty, values and integrity in order to ingratiate themselves to the ravenous corporate beast; spunking untold amounts on corporate jollys to Asian cat-houses, then discussing the profound change they experienced deep within themselves when they budgeted around the *third-world*. Pull the other leg nob-head it plays fuckin jingle bells.

Farquar wanted to visit a travel agent to look at some ticket prices. There was one on the same floor as our lodgings so I decided to tag along. We walked into to the travel agent's and Farquar sat next to me at the desk. There was a massive pile of Hong Kong dollars sitting between the travel agent and me, so I asked the travel agent how much a return ticket to Tokyo was. The daft git gets up from the desk and walks over to ask someone else about ticket prices. I swiftly pocketed most of the cash. He came back and sat down, not even noticing the huge dent I had made in his pile of money. Poor Farquar was kakking himself! He was shaking with fear as I kindly thanked the travel agent and walked out of the shop.

"What if they find out? What if they called the police?"

What if? ... What if? ...

He said he was really nervous and scared because he was a terrible liar, and was worried that the police might come and question us. I gave him a couple of quid and told him to relax. Even if the guy did tell the police, it didn't matter. The travel agent didn't even know my name. How would the police find us, when there were sixteen floors to choose from and all teeming with travellers? I told him just to keep his gob shut that if the *old bill* asked then just tell them *'I aint seen nuffink guvnor.'* Farquar looked a bit pouty and I could tell he didn't want to play with me anymore.

I took the *Star Ferry* to Hong Kong Island and spent all the stolen money in the big department stores, buying jeans, a sports bag, sunglasses, and anything else that I needed. I was in a hurry to get the money spent just in case somebody wanted it back.

I arrived back at *Chun King Mansions* laden with goods and was shocked to find the whole building crawling with uniformed cops, some of whom had machine guns. I asked one of them what was happening and he said there had been a bomb scare so they were searching every room. I met up with Farquar later, who told me he had been asleep in his room when he was woken up by two cops holding machine guns. He had confessed everything, saying that it was me who had stolen the money and that he had nothing to do with it. The cops didn't know what the hell he was talking about so they left him alone. *Stay cool. Hang loose. Admit nothing!*

16

CHASING THE DRAGON

ALL THAT SHOPPING had given me a terrible thirst. Farquar had declined the offer of joining me for a couple of beers, so I went off by myself for what was meant to be a swift half. It must have been a good night because I can't really remember what happened, but I do know I scored a strawful of white powder from some Chinese bloke outside the Seven Eleven on Nathan Road. He told me it was coke, but luckily I burned a bit on some Jimmy Boyle before I shoved it up my hooter. Charlie my arse, it was skag, and not a bad wee drop of the hard stuff it was either.

I wandered from bar to club and back again, covering all of Kowloon, which means *nine dragons* in Chinese. Hong Kong was teeming with either backpackers or stuck-up expatriates, and never the twain shall meet. I wasn't interested in either party. After a couple of hours of aimless wandering, I ended up with a lovely, wee Chinese whore on my arm, who wanted to go back and get the business over and done with. I felt like having a few more bevvies first so I took her to a pub called the *Hogs Breath* that was near the *Chun King Mansions. Madame Butterfly* said she didn't want to drink, she wanted sex. I think it was a *she*, but you have to be on your lookout in Asia. There are chicks with dicks everywhere and, *quelle horeur,* a surprise up every skirt. I talked her into having one more drink.

The pub was full of Chinese men, (as a lot of Hong Kong pubs are!), making me feel like I was in some sort of cowboy movie, swaggering into a saloon bar with the doors swinging to and fro behind me. Chinese men make no secret of the fact that they don't like seeing their girls with *gwailos* (foreign devils). Ordering a couple of drinks, my *Madame Butterfly* and I went and sat at a table in the corner. Every one in the pub was giving me the eyeball so I decided to stagger off for a leak and a chase of the dragon on the island of nine. Locked inside the toilet I poured a spot of white powder on a bit of Arthur Conan Doyle and heated it with a lighter. With a rolled-up Hong Kong banknote in my mouth, I chased the smoke and sucked it deep into my lungs. When I came out of the karzee I saw a Chinese guy leaning over the table talking to my new missus. Thinking that he must know her, I left them alone and went up to the bar to order.

Enough time had elapsed for them to have their little chat, so I walked back toward the table with the drinks, and that's when I saw the snarl on his face. His finger was pointing at me as he hissed some Asian insult at her. She stood up and threw a drink over him. Immediately he took the beer glass from her hand and slammed it right into her pretty young face. The blood was everywhere. She must have had a thousands cuts all round her nose, mouth and eyes.

Amidst the confusion some people were giving her towels to try to stop the flow of blood and helping her towards the door. *Glassman* had blood all over his clothes. With a bit of the broken glass still in his hand, he started shouting at me. I fucked two quick shots to his head, and knocked him to the floor. This brought almost the whole pub to its feet, and it looked like I was going to get it from the *Mongol hordes*. Before anyone else could step in, the *Glassman* got up and started giving it the big one, telling everyone to get out of the way; that he would have me himself. Still groggy from the first two hits I'd landed, he tried a *Kung Fu* kick to my head. I managed to duck under his flying legs and hit him with a left hand to the temple, completely pole- axing him. He was knocked out cold, and I managed to stamp on his head a bit before some bastard hit me with a bottle. I staggered out of the pub as blows and random objects were rained down upon me. Having taken so much *smack* I didn't feel any pain so I legged it back to my fartsack and crashed out.

I woke up the next morning with the dried blood from my head wound sticking my face to the pillow. It was hard to get my jeans off because the blood had stuck them to my legs. I wasn't sure how I had acquired the cuts on my legs, though I had a vague recollection of being knocked over by a taxi on the way home after trying to score another strawful of *smack* for a nightcap. Like I said, it must have been a good night!

My hand had swollen up like a balloon and my head needed stitches, so I decided I better see a doctor. I went to the casualty department at some big hospital and waited in line. Eventually I was looked at by this horrible little nurse who started pulling on my broken hand and poking around the cuts on my head, asking me what had happened. When I told her somebody had hit me with a bottle she gave me a look of pure disgust, then demanded to see my Hong Kong residency card before I could be treated for free. I told her I had left it at home but she was having none of it.

"No Hong Kong residency, no free treatment!"

After she'd stuck a token bandage around my hand and some gauze on my head, I wandered off to find the immigration office to register for residency.

17

TOFFS

HONG KONG WAS still a British colony at that time, so all that was required to get residency status were a couple of photographs and a British passport. On my arrival at the immigration office, there was a large crowd of Chinese people queuing outside. The office was closed for lunch, but it would be opening again in ten minutes. I took my place at the end of the line, looking a wee bit worse for wear from the previous night's shenanigans, my injured parts still bandaged and bloody.

Not long after my arrival this white guy, smartly dressed in a pin stripe suit, ignoring the lengthy queue, went straight to the office door and started banging loudly on it. I presumed he must have been a city broker or such like, because was making a big show of trying to sound very important on his phone.

He was a typical product of the chinless, horsy, inbred set - probably inbred with a horse! A Chinese security guard responded to his impatient banging and pointed to the end of the line with his stick. *Rupert* the *Horse-face* was having none of it.

"Can't you hurry up? I am a very busy man!"

He obviously wasn't too keen on the idea of hanging out with Chinese peasants in immigration offices. Even so, the guard ignored his offhand manner and closed the door in his face, leaving 'poor' *Rupert* in a fluster. Red-faced and irritated, he kept looking at his *Rolex*, continually checking the time and barking orders into his phone. His clipped 1940s *BBC* announcer voice made me want to poke him in the eye. Eventually the door to the immigration office opened and the Chinese throng jostled each other to gain entry. At the end of the room there were two desks with officials sitting behind them. I joined one queue *and Horse-face* joined the other. He was about six people behind me. When it came to my turn I put my passport and pictures on the desk, however the woman official told me that I was in the wrong line. I needed to join the other line for the required finger printing, which had be done first! The thought of having to queue up again behind *Rupert* did not appeal, so I smiled, bowed, and ingratiated myself with the people in the other line. The fawning strategy worked, as I was allowed to take up position in front of *Rupert*. None of the officials or other people in the line seemed to mind what they considered a simple mistake by a foreigner. *Horse-face* had, of course, taken it as a personal affront; *how could a scumbag such as I dare to jump in front of one as up himself as he?* He was now snapping his fingers in an attempt to draw my attention. Of course I ignored him. Not to be deterred, he turned up the volume on his nobby accent.

"I say, young man! I'm addressing you! Hey, you there with the bandaged head!".

His toffee-nosed protestations were making my peasant blood boil. Surely to Christ I could be forgiven this one wee queue jump. Hadn't he and those of his ilk had it their way for long enough? From yir ethnic cleansing at the *Glencoe Massacres*, to the *Slaughter of Culloden*, to the stamping across the pages of history in muddy jodhpurs, chasing the poor wee foxes. Isn't it time we had break from it all? Us and the poor wee foxes. Hadn't you already had your pint of blood *Rupert*?

"Beck of the queue young man, I say, beck of the queue, what!"

Why is it that the British have this anal obsession for lining up? For order and discipline, for taking one's rightful place, bowing and scraping, genuflecting and saluting? Be mindful to *get on yir knees and thank Jesus at the end of the day for each crumb that should fall from Rupert's table.*

"Look mate, I'm busy right now, do you mind if I ignore you some other time? Here's two bob, go and phone somebody that gives a fuck!"

Rupert was not proving to be popular with the Chinese. They could see right through this tosser who had taken their island from its rightful owners for interrupting the good old British imperial drug trade. The thing that got my goat was that *Rupert* was oblivious to their reactions. Here he was on the other side of the world, snapping his fingers, and expecting all and sundry to come running to his beck and call; labouring under the misconception that he had saved them from their savage selves. Uncivilized tribes dropping like flies, the Picts and the Gaels, the red man and the yellow man and don't forget those fucking African savages. *'Hip, hip hurrah for Rupert!'*

Around the globe they marched, destroying the depraved opponents of civilization itself. Committed only to benevolence; spreading liberty and happiness on a noble enterprise of conquering, catechizing, uplifting and *Christianizing* the misguided savage hordes. Introducing churches, brothels, schools, opium, gonorrhea, syphilis and slavery. A great big globe painted red and governed for its own good by the Anglo-Saxon race.

"I say young man, if you don't move I will have to call security!"

Typical snotty nosed wanker! Not man enough to do anything himself, having to enlist the help of the hirelings, the goons, police constable *Flat-foot* and the Keystone Porcinistas. Society's bouncers in monkey suits, clutching their bananas and protecting the rich. If this had been Britain, my feet wouldn't have touched the ground. I would have been wheeched off to the *Tower* by some stout yeomen of the guard for a swift beheading. This wasn't the UK however and Hong Kong was soon to be returned to China. The underpaid security guards didn't really appreciate that *Rupert* had brought them freedom and democracy. Whether in a monarchy, a democracy, or a dictatorship of the proletariat, these security guards would always remain on starvation wages, so they couldn't really give a monkeys about *Rupert's* little hissy fit. His noisy protestations fell on deaf ears, his Empire crumbled and in ruins!

18

EASTERN TRAFFIC

RETURNING TO MY fleapit hostel, I realised that in my muddled haste to receive medical attention, I had left my door wide open, and some enterprising tea-leaf had made off with whatever meager belongings I had possessed. Luckily I was sporting a nifty little bum-bag with the bare essentials (i.e. passport and money), so all was not lost. One of the staff suggested calling the police, but a fat lot of good they have ever been. The last thing I needed was some twat in a clown uniform asking silly questions. The shock of losing my belongings called for a hair-of-the-dog and a game of pool at the local Seaman's Club. The Seaman's Club was a well known den of iniquity, and was a popular recruiting spot for smuggler's mules. After a few drinks I fell in with a posse of dodgy English blokes who began to fill me in on the smuggling coup. They suggested trying a quick milk-run to earn a bit of cash. A milk-run is a euphemism for a smuggling trip. The Triads make money by smuggling goods into various countries and avoiding the import tax.

They gave me a few contacts, and within the week I had set myself up with a *run*. I was part of a group of maybe ten to twenty backpackers; we would all travel together on the same plane. The route was Hong Kong to Taiwan to Korea, then Korea back to Hong Kong. The booty consisted of two *walkmans*, expensive *Nikon* camera equipment, a video camera, gold jewellery, and some other shite that wasn't so significant.

The next afternoon the group boarded a flight to Taipei. We had been told by the people who organised the trip that in the event customs searched our bags they would stamp our passports. This would state that the items were brought into the country, with the proviso that on leaving the country we had to still have these goods with us. When we arrived we all went through the line marked '*Nothing to declare*'. A couple of the group were stopped but most of us walked through unhindered.

I can't remember the shite they put in my suitcase, but the first part of the journey from Hong Kong to Taiwan was a breeze and I sailed through customs. I think I was given about fifty dollars for expenses, plus the ticket, hotel and a lump sum. There were a lot of skint backpackers in Asia; this was a way of making a couple of quid. What could go wrong? If customs find the booty they stamp it in your passport. If they don't, you make some money. Totally risk-free, apparently.

At Seoul airport things started to go a wee bit pear-shaped. One of the customs guards was eyeing me suspiciously.

"Have you got anything to declare?"

I looked around then pointed at myself as if surprised that he was talking to me.

"Who? Me?"

"Yes, you! Do you have a *walkman*? Any electrical goods? A video camera? Gold? Guns or drugs?"

"No. Nothing to declare."

He opened my suitcase and looked at the assortment of electrical goods; video cameras, a *walkman*, a *Nikon* 501 with telephoto lens and another *walkman* I had hidden in a sock.

"I thought you didn't have any electrical equipment?"

This customs man was evidently wise to this scam and probably sussed that I was part of an organised smuggling ring.

"Do you have any gold?"

"No, Sir."

He had everything else, so there was no way I was going to let on I had a gold bar on a chain around my neck, thus foregoing the opportunity of earning fifty dollars.

"Come this way, please."

He guided me through a metal detector and the inevitable happened. It went off, burping an electronic beep. I was searched and forced to hand over the gold bar, then I was taken to the airport lockup. I was questioned by the *old bill* and told that smuggling gold was a serious offence in Korea. I could face up to four years in prison. So much for a *milk-run* being totally safe!

There I was, sitting at this desk in the police station, giving them my pathetic excuses about not knowing any better, when a Korean guy was dragged in wearing handcuffs. It was difficult not to overhear him explain nervously that he had flown in on a flight from Thailand, when two big bags of white powder were unceremoniously plonked in front of him. The police were shouting at him, punching him in the ribs and slapping him about the kisser; pointing accusingly at the white powder. He was handcuffed so he couldn't put up much of a fight even if he'd wanted to. A stubble-headed mean monster of a cop grabbed the sorry looking bastard a little too firmly around the neck. He started choking, his lips turning greyish blue as he gasped for air. He looked as though he was going to bite the bullet when the stubble-head dropped him. He fell, choking for breath, to the floor. The sad bastard just lay there crying, trying to cover his head from the slaps, punches and kicks that the pigs were giving him. He seemed too frightened to speak, only replying by nodding his head whenever they asked him a question. Following one of their numerous questions he started shaking his head in denial. He either didn't know or he did not want to answer. They were probably asking him whom he was working for. That was the last I saw or heard of him as they marched me off to the cells.

Four police officers were in the cell with me. They gestured, indicating I should sit down on a wicker chair that had seen better days, and was guaranteed to give an itchy arse to any poor bastard forced to park his buns on it. Just like in the movies, the cops opted for the *good guy, bad guy* approach, and the *good guy* offered me an fag which was gratefully accepted. A hefty dose of tar on the lungs is always good for the nerves and this particular brand of Korean salmon certainly did the trick. Whilst contemplating my fate in a cloud of smoke, I happened to notice one of them beginning to remove his belt.

"Who you work for?"

It is often read of in the tabloids; of extremely heroic people who have suffered savage beatings at the hands of heartless captors because they wanted to keep some closely guarded secret from falling into enemy hands. Bullet-proof respect goes out to those brave courageous people! Me, myself and I, on the other hand, immediately told them the names of the two guys I was working for and the address of the hotel where we were to meet them. They locked me in the cell for the night; it was colder than a witch's tit. I had always thought of Korea as some warm, exotic place but there you go.

The light was left on all night; the old sleep deprivation, a psychological approach to wear the prisoner down and make him more open to suggestion. Completely unnecessary in my case as I was prepared to *sing like a canary*. In the morning, the cops returned, handing me a cup of tasteless coffee and a much needed cancer stick. The deal was that they would hang on to all my belongings, while I would go to the hotel where the two Hong Kong *Triads* were staying and get one thousand US dollars. Then they would give back the goods. I rode a cab to the centre of Seoul and located the two *Triads*. This was a normal occurrence in *milk-runs* and they didn't seem to mind. They gave me the thousand bucks and told me that the Koreans would deport me back to Hong Kong, but that they would give me back the goods in question. I was to go to the *Triads'* software shop in Hong Kong and hand back the goods to the staff working there.

When I returned to the police station and, sticking to my part of the deal, delivered the money, they immediately locked me up again. I sweated it out for a while, however, true to the *Triads'* word, I found myself in the very fortunate position of being deported back to Hong Kong, luggage and booty returned to me!

Two policemen escorted me, handcuffed, onto the plane. Upon finding my seat and sitting down, they released me from the cuffs, handed me my passport, complete with a fresh Korean deportation order stamp, then left without as much as a by-your-leave. The other passengers on the plane avoided my gaze for the whole flight, probably thinking I was a big hard criminal. But I'm sure the *trolley dollies* were gagging for it, secretly lusting to join the *mile high club* with public enemy number one.

I enjoyed my fifteen minutes of fame, staring down the businessmen like the renegade outlaw I was. *They seek him here... They seek him there... That dammed elusive Pimpernel!* Maybe it was all in my head; perhaps the stewardesses knew after all that I was just a humble *walkman* smuggler. It could have been worse though, I could have been wearing lycra shorts and been branded as a grape smuggler.

19

LOVE ME TENDER

THE SMUGGLING BUG had definitely got to me. Never before had I experienced such intense highs and lows in such a short space of time. Now a fully-fledged adrenalin junkie, I hungrily sought my next fix. As in any Asian city with a transient population of naïve, Caucasian, budget-travellers, Hong Kong comes equipped with a group of ne'er-do-wells just waiting to exploit this commodity. Take any skint Caucasian budget traveller, give him a shower and shave, dress him up in some clean clothes, and hey presto - he will pass through Asian customs pretty much unhindered.

After not too much asking around on the budget traveller's grapevine, I was told to look out for a long time Hong Kong resident named Crispin, who recruited people for the smuggling gangs. He was said to frequent the canteen on the sixteenth floor of the *Chun King Mansions*. The only description I was given was that the bloke was English and gay. This description seemed rather stereotypical and I wasn't very confident that this information would be enough for me to find the him. My theory proved wrong. As soon as our eyes met over a crowded, smoky canteen I knew he was my man. Not just your common or garden variety pillow-biter, but a mincing, poncey, theatrical poof. As I walked towards his table he must have crossed and uncrossed his legs a hundred times in a fluster, wiggling about on his chair as if there was something long and sharp wedged up his rusty sheriff's badge.

"Hello *Butch*. Where have you been all my life?"

"Dundee"

"Did ya bring yir kilt hen," says the Crisp in a put-on Scots accent.

"Aye but it's in the dry cleaners noo wi ma bag-pipes."

"Ah'll bet yi can fairly blow them things *Jock*"

Eventually, after much frivolity, the Crisp and I discussed the issue at hand. He offered me a choice between two smuggling trips. One was for an Indian posse that brought gold from Hong Kong to Nepal. The other was also smuggling gold, but it was for some Chinese *Triads* who brought the gold to Taiwan.

"The Indians will dress you up like a climber and hide the gold in the hiking boots you wear on the plane," Crispin informed me.

"Must make the boots a bit heavy dunnit?"

"Big strong boy like you shouldn't have a problem."

"Done any climbing yersel' Crisp?"

"No, never been up Everest but I've been up a man that had."

We didn't have to go far too find the Indians; they were only two floors below us. After a short walk down the dingy stairway, we entered the fourteenth floor which looked and smelt like Gandhi's flip-flop. It was hot and muggy as we squeezed our way along the dark corridor. Every room we passed was filled to the gills with Indians of all shapes and sizes and in varying costumes. Dhotis and beards, incense and pujas, curries and turbans! They all looked like film extras from an *Ali Baba* movie. Crispin knocked on a door and we were let into a small room. Inside, four Indian men sat on a couple of mangy mattresses that had seen better days. There were plates of unfinished food lying around, and the smell of pungent curry was unimaginable. The men fussed over Crispin, blowing air kisses and patting his bum. They didn't look like shit-shovellers but hoo noze. These Western Oriental gentlemen never leave their friends behind. One of the men proffered a red plastic stool for me to sit on and handed me a *hashish joint*. I took a few long contemplative tokes on the old *Bob Hope* while the Crisp filled me in on the scam. He laid out everything I would need for a trekking expedition on one of the mattresses. There was a sleeping bag and a tent, some pots and pans, woolly balaclavas, warm socks etc. etc. These items all had price tags on them and were obviously the cheapest shite that money could buy. The tent was so cheap and flimsy that it wouldn't keep a mouse warm. Crispin tried to help me put on the hiking boots with the gold inside them as I held the tent up for a closer inspection of the price tag. Crispin laced the boots up and motioned for me to try and walk forwards in them. When I tried to stand up the *spliff* kicked in and I felt suddenly very light-headed. I held up the tent for Crispin to see the sale tag.

"Look Crisp, *This is the winter of our discount tents!*"

Both of us nearly collapsed with laughter, but there was no way I could even lift my feet, the boots were so fucking heavy. There was an embarrassed silence in the room as Crispin and I tried to stifle our giggles, made our excuses and left. As we headed back up to the sixteenth floor, Crispin explained to me that the bastards just kept getting greedier and putting more and more ridiculous amounts of gold in the boots. So much so that I couldn't even lift a leg. Crispin made a few free calls from a payphone in the canteen and arranged for us to meet the Chinese *Triad* gang in a restaurant just down the street on Nathan Road. We went into the restaurant and I stood behind Crispin as he made the introductions to a table of four men. The four men, who all looked remarkably similar, stood up and each one shook my hand and gave me their business cards. As far as I could gather from Crispin's introductions, their names were Mr Wong, Mr Wing, Mr Long and Mr Ling. Local telephone calls are free of charge in Hong Kong and it was now obvious, at least to me, why so many people in the colony frequently *ling the long number.*

Mr Wong (or was it Wing) began to explain the smuggling run to me. Apparently, it was a cinch, as the Taiwanese government was trying to beef up the *Won* by piling up the gold reserves. Hence the reason why the Taiwanese customs officers were in on the scam, and according to Wong there wasn't much risk. The flight was only about an hour long, and for each run the reward was a thousand US dollars in cash. Crispin gave me a good reference and I was hired.

The next morning Mr Wing accompanied me on a shopping mission. We ended up in a large well-known department store where he bought shiny new 'smart but casual' shoes, some black trousers and a shirt and tie. Last but not least a silver coloured suit jacket! Ours is not to reason why, but a silver fucking jacket, I ask you? However, one had to suffer some indignity. The *Triads* obviously had a character in mind for me to depict, and besides, I needed the dough. The situation was comical nonetheless. The shop assistant was attempting to find a jacket that actually fitted me, and couldn't understand why Mr Wing was insisting on one almost three sizes larger than necessary. Little did he know that it was to enable the secreting of the gold that was to be strapped about my chest. This fact hadn't been worked out by myself yet either, as I was agreeing totally with the extremely confused shop assistant that the silver jacket fitted like a tent. Perhaps I was going to climb Everest after all! The *Triad* was very persuasive, and the extra large silver jacket was chosen. My previous assumptions that smugglers were supposed to be discreet had now been blown away; all I would need to complete my ensemble were some glass slippers and a great big pumpkin on my head.

Lunch with the other *Triads* in a nearby restaurant followed the shopping mission. Mr Wing seemed quite pleased with the clothes he had chosen for me. I hadn't realised just how little English Mr Wong understood until I asked him a few questions over lunch concerning the run. He just answered yes to everything. He even nodded enthusiastically when I asked him if he had ever been blindfolded with dental floss, which worried me no end. And how on earth people of such small stature can eat so much in such a small space of time I shall never know. These guys would have eaten the arse out of a low flying duck if one had flown by. After gorging ourselves on some unrecognizable, greasy but not unpleasant dead animals, Wong paid the bill and we walked out to the street and hailed a cab.

We rode back to his place where a group his underlings were preparing for the forthcoming trip. This assortment of fearsome looking Chinese punters were packing suitcases and yelling orders at each other. They turned and looked at me as if I was some kind of sacrificial lamb going to the alter. They all had what I call the *Asian Face*, that solemn impassivity associated with the Oriental demeanor. A non-committal '*Go fuck yourself, Foreign Devil'* type of look. A couple of them did manage to smile but they were crocodiles smile. Even the big scabby dog that was lounging in the corner of the room growled at me when I tried to pat him. What struck me as odd was that the expression in the dog's eyes never changed even when he growled; the dog too had the *Asian Face*.

One of the goons could speak a bit of *Chinglish*, trying in a haphazard fashion to explain the plan of action. He looked a bit like a fat Chinese *Elvis* having a big hair day, wearing winkle-pickers, black razor creased slacks and a fifties-style cowboy shirt with a bootlace tie round his neck. His job would be to accompany me on the plane. Not exactly, what one would call a match made in heaven; *MacCinderella* and a Chinese Rock-a-Billy rebel. Talk about the odd couple.

Between us we were to carry four expensive looking suitcases. I also had a leather briefcase and a holster type belt thing to attach to my chest for a portion of the 28 kilos of gold. The rest was wrapped in Christmas wrapping paper and strewn around inside my luggage. This is how the gold was going to be transported through the airport. What the wrapping paper was all about I have no idea because it was nowhere near Christmas.

Elvis was to leave a bag containing the bars of gold in the toilet situated in the airport departure lounge for me to collect. The bag and its contents then stayed with me, as I was to take the bag onto the plane. Due to the flight only being an hour long, the transfer of the bars to my person had to be carried out early in the journey. The plane's toilet would be used to transfer the bars to the holster which I would then strap around my chest, concealing it under cover of the larger-than-life silver *Cinderella* jacket. It had to be done before the meal was served, as in all probability the toilet would be in full use afterwards.

When we arrived in Taiwan, *Elvis* would make a telephone call to find out the aisle number our customs man was going to be working on. *Courvoisier* brandy and green menthol cigarettes had to be purchased and put on top of my luggage trolley. This would indicate to our customs man that I was the person with the contraband

and that he should get me through as quickly as possible.

It all seemed pretty straightforward, as long as I didn't
get too pissed on the flight. It should have been a cake-
walk, but as the great Bard said, *'The best laid plans of
mooses and men gang aft astray.'* There I stood, done up
like a haggis, the great chieftain o' the pudding race.

20

CURLY SLIPPERS

WE WENT TO the airport and I picked up the bag that Elvis had left for me in the departure lounge toilet. Inside were the bars of gold, the holster and clothes. I had started feeling paranoid already, walking into the toilet with nothing and coming out with a big chunky bag.

"The *China Airlines* flight to Taiwan will be delayed for 20 minutes due to engine trouble."

The little voice inside my head started picking away at my confidence. *'They're on to you man! Engine trouble, my arse!.'* I chain smoked until the next announcement.

"All passengers on flight CA 666 to Taipei please board the aircraft."

I felt like there were a million pairs of eyes watching me. We got on the plane and my seat was between some German businessman type and an older looking Chinese housewife. A stewardess pointed to an overhead locker and told me to put the bag up there. She had to help me lift it. She laughed and said, "That's a very heavy bag. What have you got in there?"

There is a time and place for everything, and polite stewardess attempts at customer relations weren't really called for at that point. *'If I tell you I will have to kill you,'* may have been an appropriate answer on this occasion.

The plane took off and we had just got out of Hong Kong airspace when I noticed *Elvis* in the row opposite me, his hairstyle particularly bouffed for the special occasion. He had discreetly seated himself far enough away from me so that people wouldn't connect us. Soon he started signaling with his big hairstyle toward the toilet, implying I should get on with it; go to the bogs and strap some gold bars to my chest. I wasn't really in a big rush, but *El Bouffee* was becoming more and more animated and I didn't want people to realize we were both very much *at it*.

I grabbed the bag out of the over-head locker and slammed it down onto the floor below my seat. At this point I felt like the whole plane was watching me as I opened the bag. When someone opens a bag in a public place it is natural human curiosity to wonder what will be taken out of it. I had never really considered this until now, but the longer I shuffled around inside the bag pretending to look for something, the more I could feel people's eyes watching me to see what I was going to produce. I felt like a conjurer.

'Ladies and Gentlemen! As you can see, there is nothing in my hands. Now before your very eyes I will produce 15 kilograms of gold and run down to the bog and strap it to my chest without anyone knowing it! And how, Ladies and Gentlemen, am I, the great Alibaba of the curly slippers to perform this master illusion? Good question Ladies and Gentlemen! And I am sure there is a very fucking good answer to it! I just don't know what it is!'

I didn't have anything to put the bars in to take it to the toilet. What was I to do? Wrap them in some be-skidded jocks? A holey sock perhaps? I tried to keep my cool head on. What would *Bond* do in this situation?

"Relaksh Moneypenny. I have the shituashon in hand. Should preshent no shignificant problem"

97

I clunked the bars and holster into a pile and covered them with the *Cinderella* jacket, then lurched down the aisle looking like *Quasimodo*. People were staring at me; I could feel it. The old crow sitting next to me *must* have heard the clunk of the gold as I piled it up. She gave me one of those looks like she knew what the scoop was. My card was stamped. My ticket was punched. My tea was well and truly 'oot'. I considered getting *The Man From Bouffant* to flush her down the toilet.

I came out of the chantey with much expanded chest. It was very uncomfortable and very hot. By the time we got off the plane I was sweating like a pedophile at a nativity play. *Elvis* made the phone call and our man was working on aisle thirteen. I went to collect my bags from the circular conveyor belt thing. I had been told to put 'engineer' as my occupation on the customs form so that desk thirteen would recognize me. The problem was that the airport was busy and some lines were longer than others, so there was a uniformed guard re-directing people from one line to another. I didn't fancy the idea of lining up at aisle thirteen, then being shifted to aisle ten because it was empty. So I decided to let the luggage go round a few times.

The thing that really scared me was that after our man on aisle thirteen had searched the belongings of passengers, there was another uniformed guard re-checking what had just been checked. My man would give me the OK but the re-check man was bound to question the gold bars wrapped in Christmas paper strewn around my luggage. That's if I managed to get past the bloke moving people to different lines. I watched my bags go round and round. *Elvis* had already gotten through customs and was standing in front of two machine-gun-toting military policemen, motioning with his big hair for me to get on with it. It was a suicide mission but I had no choice. It was either stand there all day sweating it out at the conveyor belt with my thumb up my arse, or *kamikaze* it through aisle thirteen. I threw the bags onto the trolley and got in line.

There was a queue of about six people and the guard told me and the two guys behind me to join another line. I bent down to tie my lace and stayed where I was. My man on customs looked absolutely terrified. We were about to be rumbled! Every bag he opened and checked was opened and re-checked by another guard who was watching over him. It was all going horribly ostrich-shaped. It came to my turn and I handed over my customs form. My man had just started rifling through my things when the guard who was re-checking moved down to the next row and began to re-check somewhere else. Re-check man was in on it! He was one of us! Halleluiah! I felt like skipping gaily through the airport screaming *'Chase me ladies, I'm in the cavalry!'* My limo was waiting outside along with Mr Wong and Mr.Wing. Fuck knows what happened to *Elvis*. Apparently he had left the arena.

21

DOGGIE STYLE

AFTER A QUICK shower, me and the chaps went to celebrate my successful trip at some hostess club next to the hotel where we were staying. As we went up in the lift everyone seemed to be in a good mood, making that universal 'wee man in the boat' sign by sticking their thumbs between their first two fingers and saying "Joogy-joogy," which I suppose must have meant nookey-nookey in Chinese.

The lift reached the designated floor and opened straight into the club, and the sight that met my eyes was most welcoming. It was a big roomy club full of long red velvet couches with a stage in the centre. There was a long bar down one side of the club with a flashing neon sign in Chinese above it. The girls who worked there were all wearing these one-piece, glittering mini-skirt affairs. All had long black hair and legs that came right up to their armpits. If it wasn't for the numbers on their name badges it would have been extremely difficult to tell them apart. Any one of those sexy little uniforms would look great in a crumpled heap on my bedroom floor.

Two athletic lap dancers were doing a floorshow. They covered each other in oil and started sliding up and down a pole. Confucius say: 'Woman who slide down banister make monkey shine.'

My mojo was definitely on the rise after such an adrenalin rush at the airport, and those little babes were making me stiff as a board. A juicy game of hide-the-sausage later was definitely on the cards.

We were shown to a table. Mr Wong ordered a bottle of *Dom* and a few of the tarts joined us. Mr Wong told me to remember which numbered girl I liked best and he would arrange to have her sent up to my room later. The drunker I got the more difficult it became to pick the lucky girl. Every half-hour the girls would change to different tables, mingling with the customers. Each time a new set of nubiles would join our table, the boss insisted that one-by-one they flash their pink bits and show us what they had for breakfast.

Apparently, this was a very exclusive and expensive club and the girls had to be exceptionally pretty to work here. To be honest, they were all exceptional, and I would have dragged my balls over broken glass to hear any one of these charming young things fart through a walkie-talkie. *Elvis* had re-appeared and was loving it, groping away under the table then sticking his middle finger up my nose asking if I would like to smell his new girlfriend. I reached over, shook her hand and asked her how much her name was. She smiled and I told her she had the whitest teeth I had ever had the good fortune to 'come' across. In answer she winked and pointed at her number. It's actually quite refreshing how Asian girls don't have this *Christian* guilt thing about sex. Hump a Western girl and she will ask daft questions like, "*Do you like me?*" Shag an Asian girl and she'll ask, "*Do you like fucking me?*"

Love and lust. *Vive le difference!* I was having real problems trying to decide which number to pick when *Elvis* gestured for me to follow him to the bog. We went into a cubicle and he chopped out a couple of fat lines of white powder. I asked him what it was. He winked and told me it was a *cocktail*. Whatever it was it definitely worked. I must have been getting completely out of it because I was even attempting to sing Chinese songs on the *karaoke*. I went in to sniff more of the *cocktail* and promptly passed out in the bogs.

What an absolute tragedy! All that blart, begging to get fucked and I'm fuckin' home alone. Dirty rotten Chinese bastards! Risking my neck and what did I get for it? Some shitty drugs, a hangover and a hard-on. My eyes adjusted to the darkness of the room as I stumbled out of bed to go for a piss.

Emerging, I noticed a pair of white high heels under the bed, which as far as I could recall didn't belong to me. In the darkness I could just about make out the shape of a body under the covers. Perhaps after all I had judged too early and been a bit harsh on my colleagues. They were an alright bunch those Chinese blokes, and I wouldn't have a word said against them.

Pulling back the covers to discover the luscious honey I had ended up with; hoping for number four or six, even number seven would have done, but woe was me. The rotten filthy bastards had done me up like a kipper! She was a fucking gargoyle! *Medusa* wouldn't have had a look in here. It must have fallen from a great height out of the ugly tree and got a terrible thrashing with the ugly log. This was obviously the chappies' idea of a joke. I'm the first to admit that when it comes to sex I am not exactly choosy; *any port in a storm* and all that old tosh. Nevertheless this thing, object or whatever it was that was now prostrate in my bed, would have scared the buzzards off a meat wagon! My moral standards may have been lower than a snake's belly but this took the biscuit. This thing would have made an onion cry. I picked up the telephone.

"Hello, this is 511. I have the wrong number."

"What number were you trying for sir?"

"Any fucking number except this one!" The girl on reception hung up on me.

Galen is now awake and sitting up in bed, teeth so squint she could have eaten an apple through a tennis racquet. With my eyes closed, my mind wandered back to images of the little pole-dancers gyrating in the club earlier. Imagination is a powerful thing, and the next thing you know Galen is being hosed down in the shower. Surprisingly she looked a little better dripping wet; her jet black hair glistened in the lamplight like nose-hair after a sneeze.

I think it was her big knickers that eventually got me worked up. Remenber the good old days when you pulled down a bird's knickers to look at her arse? Nowadays you have to pull open her arse to see her knickers. The big-knicker phenomenon is almost extinct in the civilized world, where women's scanties are barely wide enough to floss your teeth with. It certainly was a sad day for sex when the big-knicker factories shut their doors and made way for more sleek, customised models. Too much too soon. Less is more. I, for one, would definitely applaud the renaissance of the large panty. *Vive les humungus undies!* Another added bonus was that her suntan stopped just below the knee, she had ticks between her toes and she left footprints on the toilet seat; all of which meant she was fresh out of the ricefield. This combination of wet hair, big drawers and ticks brought out the *Cro-magnon man* in me, and all my previous superficial thoughts were quickly forgotten. Confucius say: *'Man who put cream in tart not always baker.'*

We were at it for hours. It was a real workout. This girlie must have had more balls across her nose than a trained seal. There is definitely a lot of truth in the popular notion that female persons challenged in the looks department *aim to please*. The sex was so immensely gratifying that even the neighbours had a cigarette!

22

SHURLEY SHOME PISHTAKE

SOMETIMES IT SEEMS that when you step onto a national airline you have already reached your destination. Japan had always fascinated me and here I was, the only passenger in Business Class, Hong Kong to Tokyo. The flying waitresses were delectable. Their soft little feminine voices making the announcements that sounded like, "Wishi-washi. Wishi-washi," were getting me all worked up. They were not slow in dishing out the bevy either. We had hardly gotten out of Hong Kong air space when there was a can of ice-cold Japanese lager in my hand. 'Japanese Girl, you're a great way to fly!' As I was the only person flying Business Class, the trolley-dolly had to do the little oxygen-mask dance for my eyes only. Coooooar! What a delicate little whistle-blower she was.

Hong Kong had begun to get a bit claustrophobic and it was a relief to be moving on to greener pastures. I had seen a sign on the notice board in the *Chun King Mansions* advertising a cheap flight to Tokyo. A German girl had a round the world ticket and didn't want to use the last part, which was Hong Kong to Tokyo. Apparently she had to get back to Germany quickly, as one of her Bratwursts had exploded killing her entire family outright. I bought the ticket from her for fifteen English pounds. She came to the airport with me, checked in under her name and gave me the boarding card. When I handed in it to the immigration official, he pointed out in his halting English that the name on it read Fräulein Gabi Müller and that my passport said something completely different. There is nothing worse in my opinion than a jobsworth bureaucrat with nothing better to do than drag up this finicky red tape crap. It causes nothing but hinder and delay to those trying to go about their everyday business. Of course, I let him know in no uncertain terms that his attitude left a lot to be desired. Threatening to report him to his superiors, I grabbed the boarding pass and passport from his hands and made my way towards the waiting area. Bloody foreigners! I decided I had time to stop at the bar for some liquid refreshment before boarding the plane. After a few swift halves I heard an announcement over the PA.

"Would Miss Gabi Müller, please board the plane."

I quipped to the barman that it was unusual for a *Kraut* to be late when they are normally a nation of ardent clock-watchers. I was about to order another half when I realised that the tardy German was me! It was actually a lucky break being late because there had been an overbooking; economy was full and Fräulein Gabi Müller was upgraded to Business Class. Thank God, I didn't have to subject myself to the peasants in coach class with their elbows, knees, snotty noses, and crying babies. It was only the best for the Fräulein.

I must say I really enjoyed that flight. Apart from the luxury of Business Class, it was quite a relief to be flying without a caseload of contraband crammed in my cummerbund.

After successfully landing at Tokyo's Narita Airport, a Japanese immigration official seemed a bit put out about the fact that I didn't have an ongoing ticket out of the country. What a wanker! I had only just got there. I didn't see how or when I was leaving was any concern of this lackey. I brought his attention to the demeaning signs in English that indicated one line for Japanese returning home and the other line for *'Aliens'*. I have been called a lot of names in my life but this association with extra terrestrials was beyond the pale. Blatant discrimination! Here he was, pestering me with questions about my financial resources and I had to enter his country as an *alien*. What happened to the good old days when the sun never set on the British Empire? Then again that was only because nobody would trust the English in the dark.

23

OLAL SEX

I MADE MY way to the trains and located the Ueno Express to central Tokyo. The Japanese train system is efficient, punctual, and best of all, it must be the easiest country in the world to get a free ride. There are probably outlets for buying tickets but I never really looked for them. I had an address of a Gaijin house nearby a train station called Yoyogi Uehara. Gaijin means foreigner or person from outside the country. Gaijin-san. Mr Outsider. I arrived at the station and approached several Japanese people and showed them the address.

The problem with addresses in Japan is that house numbers are not given out in numerical order. Instead they are given out as the houses are built. For example, Number 1 *Yoyogi Uehara* Street might be right next door to Number 100 *Yoyogi Uehara* Street, depending on when the house was built. It is so confusing that even the postmen have to ring twice.

Uehara means 'upper stomach', which is a mighty peculiar name for a train station. There were lots of weird names for underground stations in Tokyo. Names such as *Naka Meguro*, or 'the middle black eye'.

'Take the blue train to just above the stomach, and then the yellow train till you get in the middle black eye.'

I eventually found the house when I spotted a female *Gaijin* person coming down the street. She was able to show me where it was. There was an assortment of characters staying at the guesthouse from various countries. It was a boom time for the Japanese economy, so *aliens* were flooding in from far-flung corners of the globe just to get their hands on some *Yen*. The Japanese guy who ran the guesthouse showed me to my room, where I would sleep on a *futon* on the floor. I had slept on some trendy people's *futons* in the West before and they always seemed very uncomfortable and cold. Now I knew why. If you have a *futon* you need a Japanese *tatami* floor made from soft bouncy wicker-like material, not some itchy nylon carpet. It was funny to hear the Japanese guy say "Here is you whooton." The Japanese alphabet doesn't contain the letter 'F'. It's more of a 'who'. Their lips don't touch so it's not actually *'futon'*, it's 'whooton'. The Japanese alphabet has something like twenty thousand characters but no 'F'. *Silly whuckers!*

There was an assortment of long term residents in this run-down, rat-infested shit hole. An African bible-basher called Albert shared a room with a half Indian, half Scottish bloke nicknamed Yehudi McEwan. Yehudi was a real lard bucket who could put away food like you wouldn't believe. He could eat a ten course meal AND three loaves of bread. The Japanese throw away their bread crusts, so if you go into a Japanese baker's and ask for 'pan no mimi', which would translate as 'ears of bread', they give you all the crusts for free. Yehudi loved his crusty ears and he would go around all the neighbourhood bakeries mooching for them every day.

The two guys who shared my room were both English teachers. One was called Paul who came from Manchester, and the other a guy introduced himself as 'Jay Walberg the Third'. He was American, obviously. Pope John Paul or Queen Elizabeth fair enough, but 'Jay Walberg the Turd?' Give us a break! Anyway, these guys helped me put together a semblance of respectability so that I could go for English teaching job interviews. Paul lent me some 'smart but casual' Hush Puppy type shoe affairs. The Turd gave me some sensible troozirs, a cheap shirt and tie and hey presto - instant teacher!

The first thing needed was a degree. Photocopies of other people's originals were borrowed. The original names were tippexed and mine put in. Within a week I had enough academic qualifications to satisfy even the most stringent of employers. Why people waste the most fun part of their lives stuck in one of these so-called houses of learning to earn these worthless scraps of paper I will never know. My favourite, most impressive piece of paper was an MA in Linguistics from Hamburg University. I also had a BA in Performance Arts from Middlesex Polytechnic. Pity on the poor bastard that had spent four years in a leotard getting shafted up the bum by his ballet teacher, and what did he have to show for it? A BA indeed. A Big fucking Arsehole!

I eventually got a few part-time teaching jobs and the pay was really good. Something like twenty-five English pounds per hour, which was far better than a slap in the puss with a wet kipper. I had to lie about my visa status to get the job, so I told my potential employers that I was on a Japanese language study visa that allowed me to work legally. The visas and the qualifications were formalities really; the only thing the employers were concerned about was my ethnic origin. You could be the most authentically educated educator in existence, but if you are a person of colour - i.e. darkie, wog, spik - the Japanese won't have you teaching in their schools. That's not the official policy or anything but it's just the way it is. Skin pigmentation doesnt affect linguistic abilities as such, but English teaching was big business; a commercial venture. Therefore the teachers had to look authentically lily-white. Even Japanese Americans were frowned upon. The more blue-eyed and blonde-haired you were, the more chance you had of succeeding in the profession. I look more like *Pancho Villa* than a Teutonic Knight but I managed to scrape through.

The structure of most English schools was the same; a bit like battery chicken coops penned off into little sections to cram as many 'classrooms' as possible into one big room. Some desperate people were teaching an eight-hour day but I couldn't; the excruciating boredom of it was too much! There would be a fifty minute class, then the bell would ring and we would be off like *Pavlov's dogs* for a quick smoke before the next set of battery hens came in. Same old shit hour after hour.

"How are you? What are your hobbies? Have you been abroad?"

The schools charged something like five thousand US dollars a year and we had an average of seven students an hour and there were maybe fifteen foreign teachers on the floor at one time. That is a lot of dollars. The schools were popular because they advertised themselves as trendy 'conversation schools'. It was generally young Japanese girls who attended in the hope that they might meet a foreign boyfriend. It was embarrassing sometimes having a class full of girls that I had already bedded and having to ask them formal questions like "Do you have any hobbies?"

"Hai Sensei, we rike olal sex".

Confucius, he say: *"Man with tool in woman's mouth, not always dentist."*

The problem with teaching English to the Japanese is that due to cultural constraints they are not really big on conversation in their *own* language, so their attempts at English conversation were abysmal. Japanese itself isn't so much a language as a set of conditioned responses. It would be completely unthinkable and incredibly impolite for a Japanese person to strike up a meaningless conversation with a stranger in his or her own language. It is very un-Japanese to shoot the shit with a stranger.

All the lessons would start with the same daft questions. "How are you? Where do you come from? How long have you been in Japan? Do you like Japanese food?"

Then there would be an embarrassing silence and I would have to get the colouring pencils out or sometimes *Join the Dots*. My favourite was *Hang Man*, it would waste hours. I'd give them impossible ones like 'Zimbabwe' or 'xylophone'. I suppose I have had worse jobs than playing *Hang Man* for thirty quid an hour, but I was beginning to question where all this was leading.

24

SUBMERGED IN THE SUBCULTURE

MY TOURIST VISA was up but I wanted to stay in Japan longer, so I enrolled in a Japanese language school called Edo Gakko, which was full of foreign workers from developing countries. The Japanese government officially allowed foreign language students to work part-time. This was a clever ploy by the xenophobic government by which a ready supply of cheap labour was granted temporary residency in Japan to perform menial tasks that the Japanese people didn't want to do. By granting these people part-time study visas they could, at any time, fuck off all of them back to where they came from without as much as a by your leave. None of this political asylum shite in Nippon. 'Oot! And bide oot, ya thurd wurld pot-scrubbers yis.' The wages in Japan were a lot higher than India or the Philippines for instance, and lot of these people worked all the hours God sent, and would turn up at school knackered having been up all night washing dishes or cleaning toilets. Of those that attended the school, a lot were of Iranian, Nepalese, Israeli or Chinese descent. One Iranian classmate of mine called Meidi was a lovely bloke who had a glass eye. He had this unnerving habit of winking at you with his good eye. During our first lesson the teacher, Kumi–san, showed us photographs of famous people and we had to decide whether we liked them or not. The teacher would point to a celebrity's photo on the blackboard and ask,

"Konno hito suki deska? Do you like this person?"

We had to answer either 'yes' or 'no' in Japanese. It was quite a laugh; a number of people would like the individual indicated, and others wouldn't; such as the American President who proved unpopular with the majority of the class. This exercise created a light-hearted atmosphere and it was a good ice-breaker. When Kumi-san produced a picture of Yassar Arafat, the Jews and Arabs in the class howled with laughter. Being so far away from our homes and from their troubles, these sessions tended to draw people from all cultures together. When Kumi-san produced a picture of Ayatollah Khomeni, I, stupid insensitive wanker that I am, responded instantaneously with, "Yes, I like him."

Medei immediately went off his nut at my remark.

"You like this man? I lost my eye because of this man!"

He sprang up from his chair and dived over a table trying to grab me by the neck. Two of his Iranian mates jumped in and pulled him off me. He was very angry and rightly so. So typical of some ignorant wanker like me from some cushy Western democracy to think I can throw my two bobs worth in on extremely sensitive issues that I knew nothing about. I didn't say it to wind him up or anything. It was just one of those times when you put your foot in your mouth. What was the expression? *A closed mouth gathers no feet.*

Of course, after our little fracas we were both sent to see the head of the school to explain our behaviour. The old boy that ran the school was a very chilled about the whole affair. He made us pump mitts and promise to behave ourselves in future. He had to deal with these international incidents quite often and didn't seem to be very put out by it. As it was down to my insensitivity I offered my apology to Medei and he accepted.

Kumi-san would give the class homework which I would never turn in. It was my way of objecting to the type of Japanese that was being taught to us, which in my opinion was too antiquated for everyday life. The Japanese themselves never actually spoke to each other in such outdated speech. Men's Japanese and Women's Japanese are completely different and the way that they were teaching us to speak was not only effeminate; it was super polite, old granny Japanese. Totally impractical, horribly complicated and completely useless when it came to washing dishes or frying hamburgers, which was what most of the students did in the real world.

The curriculum needed to be changed; enough of this polite honorific defunct throwback to old *Samurai* days, when you got your head chopped off for forgetting to bow. As usual it was just me who was stirring up the problem really; most were quite happy to learn this polite, useless crap, wash dishes, and send home money to feed their families at the end of the month. The point had to be made though; the curriculum needed to be adapted to the present day and I saw myself as the people's champion; the spokesman for these poor creatures from far flung countries where to question authority was to invite certain death.

The real reason of my causing a hoo-ha to have the curriculum changed wasn't because I really gave a monkey's about the content of the course. It was simply because the more class time I took up arguing about the teaching, the less time I would have to spend learning. Almost every sentence in Japanese begins with an apology. *'Sumimasen,'* or, *'Terribly sorry, but...'* It was an East meets West dilemma I suppose. Or maybe even a class thing. Some posh people start every sentence with an apology. *'Terribly sorry old chap, would you be so kind as to...'* etc etc.

The Japanese language has three different alphabets; *Hiragana, Katakana* and *Squiggles*. I think the correct name for the third and largest alphabet is *Kanji,* however they all look like *squiggles* to me. The problem with the *Squiggles* is that, not only do they all look the same, but you have to draw them in a certain mathematical order. There might be seven *squiggles* in one character and they have to be drawn in order. *Squiggle* one upward. *Squiggle* two downward.

Sometimes Kumi-san would ask me to copy certain *Squiggles* on the blackboard and all the class would laugh at me because I had drawn them in the wrong order. I couldn't see what the big deal was, as the end result was the same. If my *Squiggle* eventually ended up looking like her *Squiggle* then what business was it of hers the method I employed to gain the end result? The situation was getting personal. This teacher, woman, person, thing, was overstepping the mark here and taking liberties. Bring it on Kumi-san!

It wasn't that I was abject at learning Japanese itself. Being a lover of languages, any language, everywhere I went I would do my best to converse in the local dialect. Except perhaps with Newcastle, a dialect that is completely incomprehensible to the human ear. But learning *Squiggles* was more like learning mathematics than language, and maths was never my strong point. I don't like numbers. Never have and never will. Spelling has always been my strong point as any fule knoze.

25

MAGICAL PANTY KNICKERS

I WAS SETTLING into the routine. School in the mornings, work in the afternoons, then out partying in the evening. Roppongi was the party or nightlife area of Tokyo. There was only one official disco in Tokyo at that time, called Lexington Queen and it was crap. There was a 'no dancing' law in effect in Tokyo at the time. Apparently someone somewhere had been injured while dancing, so the super safety conscious Japanese outlawed it. Plenty of bars played music but as far as dancing went it was out of the question. No-one was quite sure what legally constituted a dance or how many continuous arse jiggles a minute would be considered illegal, so the law itself caused some hilarious run-ins with the Japanese old bill.

There was one underground club called *Cleo's*; excellent music, everyone off their trolleys, and tons of cute Japanese girlies looking for foreign boyfriends. *Cleo's* was actually posing as a restaurant and every now and then, usually around two or three in the morning, the coppers would suddenly appear out of nowhere; running down the stairs with video cameras trying to catch on film someone in the lurid act of shaking a tail feather.

The members of staff were well trained. No sooner had the coppers been spotted, the staff they would quickly shut off the music, pull chairs and tables onto the dance floor, and lower down a movie screen. A film would start playing and the house lights would be turned up. The coppers would then run around looking for evidence of people having danced, for example sweating bodies or shaking hips, and would film them. It was ludicrous to be sitting at a table next to a complete stranger with your eyes popping out your head in the glare of lights, trying to look interested in some daft movie whilst a Japanese policeman filmed your chest and heavy breathing.

The Japanese media held foreign influences responsible for the crumbling moral state of Japanese society, and arse wiggling was lambasted in the dailies as euphoric devil worship. The movement wasn't crushed though, it just went underground. Japanese arses aren't really made for wiggling anyway. They are very linear as far as arses go. That's why Japanese woman buy these heavily padded panties to make their bums more spherical. Ironic really, as most women go to terrific lengths to make their arses appear smaller; jumping off wardrobes or using shoehorns to fit into tight jeans.

Japanese people are taught from a very young age to sit in a position they call 'cesa', where they sit on their heels with legs bent at the knees. They do it in *Martial Arts* classes or flower arranging classes or even on the bus, sitting in this position for hours without moving and seemingly without pain. Generations of sitting in that strange position has given them these uniquely flat, shapeless, straight white legs. The Japanese expression for this is '*daikon ashi*'. *Ashi* means legs and a *daikon* is a long straight thick radish.

My spoken Japanese was coming along and I would try out my newly learned expressions on Kumi-san. She wasn't impressed and I resented her treating me like a little schoolboy. Here I was working and studying on the other side of the world, earning more money than she was, and I would get a telling-off for forgetting my pencil. My Japanese language abilities may not have been as good as they could have been but her English wasn't that great either. She asked me why I had to be late every day and I told her in my excellent Japanese that the reason I was late every day was because I was that kind of guy.

"So yu ninjin daro."

What I had actually said was, "I am that kind of carrot."

Ningen is person. *Ninjin* is carrot. She had a good laugh at that one. Bitch! I asked her how to say '1,000 fisherman' in Japanese and she answered before she realised that *'senzuri'* has two meanings; 1,000 fisherman or wanker. Usual childish crap. She asked if any one could play a musical instrument and I said *'saguhatchi'*, which is a Japanese flute but it also means blowjob.

The big test was coming up soon and everyone in the classroom knew that I was doomed to failure. The test was to be a written one and I couldn't write in Japanese. If I didn't pass I was to be put back in the dummy's class. I didn't mind being put back to the remedial class, as I wasn't destined for an academic career anyway, but I didn't want this bitch gloating, knowing that she had finally got one over on me.

The day before the test Kumi-san was bursting with excitement. Everyone was nervous and asking her all kinds of questions on *Squiggle* formations. As it was the school that sponsored us, the rumour was that if anyone failed their exams it could endanger their visas. I was of the impression that the rumour was just a ploy to keep the dishwashers and noodle-shop workers in a state of fear so they would toe the line. Anyway, what were they going to do? Banish me to a penal colony in leg irons all because I couldn't *Squiggle*? The pressure was on but I was cool as a cucumber. She told the class to attend nice and early in the morning, but made a point of singling me out for further humiliation by suggesting I come earlier than anyone else because I would have so much more work to do. Then she asked me if I was looking forward to going back to the dummies.

I woke up with a stonking hangover on the day of the test and decided against going in for my public humiliation. I was happy enough to be demoted to the dummies, but she wanted blood, and insisted I do the exam the next day just to put the boot in. I thought this was completely unnecessary but she wouldn't be deterred. The exam results were to be posted on the notice board and Kumi-san wanted public embarrassment for me. A big round zero beside my name, boldly displayed for all and sundry to see.

Kumi-san had given back the already marked exam papers and everyone was sitting around discussing their competent *Squiggology*. The class swot was a girl who sat next to me, so when she wasn't looking I whipped her exam paper, ran next door to the photocopy shop and copied it. I managed to get it back on her desk before anyone noticed. Who was going to gloat now then, *Radish Legs?*

The next morning she sat me in a little room by myself and presented me with the exam paper, telling me I had one and a half hours to finish it. She shifted backwards out of the room, bowing benignly and making little "*wi-shi-washi*" noises. I took out the stolen copy with all the right answers and painstakingly copied every *Squiggle* on to my exam paper. I didn't actually know what it said but it wasn't the content that I cared about. I just wanted to see her face when I got every answer right! When time was up and she came back to pick up my exam.

Japanese people don't believe in public displays of emotion. To do so would be to lose face. She had kittens, man! There was steam coming out of her nose and ears as she jumped up and down accusing me of all kinds of things. She said I must have cheated. Me cheat, what a cheek! I told her she better be careful with her accusations. I had worked and studied hard for this exam and would not have my thunder stolen. She said I should admit I had cheated because there was no way I could have written this exam paper. There was no way she was getting the better of me on this one. I had passed with flying colours and there was nothing she or anybody else could do about it. Kumi-san left the room fuming, holding my exam paper in her hand.

The head of the school came back ten minutes later with my paper in his hand. He suggested that I apologize to *Radish Legs*. I maintained with *faux* outrage that since day one in her class, she had taken every opportunity to defile my good name, and she was now accusing me, *petit little moi*, of cheating. This was outrageous!

He asked me to read the question and answer to number three. I refused. I told him I had done the exam. It was my handwriting and I didn't see the point in discussing the matter further. This was obviously a personal issue and was blatant victimisation. I had proved myself to be a bastion of morality in this Godless society with my impeccable behaviour, and would stand for no more slurs 'pon my honour by oath!

He then said, "OK. Do you mind if I read question three to you?"

"Be my guest."

He recited question number three.

"Can you tell us something about your childhood?"

He then read my answer.

"When I was a little girl, growing up in Israel ..."

I wanted to put my Turkish slippers on for a good old-fashioned toe cringe. I thought about brass necking it further and claiming to really have been born a female in Israel, then had a sex change and moved to the UK. But it wasn't worth it. When all is said and done, more is often said, so drawing on my fine command of the language, I said nothing.

26

BROWN TROUT

THE GUESTHOUSE I was staying at was full of hostesses. There were lots of jobs earning good money for foreign girls working in Japanese hostess bars. Japan is an incredibly chauvinistic society and Japanese men don't stand around in pubs like normal blokes talking to their mates about boxing, football or whatever. Japanese geezers go to hostess bars where they are entertained by girls, either Western or Japanese.

It's not exactly prostitution, but the girls have to pamper the men's egos, pour their drinks and flash their knickers. Whether they sleep with the man or not is their own decision. It's a macho thing with Japanese men. They would offer astronomical amounts of money just to bed foreign women. There was one French girl from my *Gaijin* house whose name was Jill. She got paid the equivalent of six thousand English pounds, a round-trip ticket to Hawaii and a diamond necklace just to sleep with a Japanese doctor who was so old that he couldn't get it up anyway. She would always arrive home drunk at three in the morning, so frustrated at having her fanny groped by little creepy businessmen that she would stagger into my *futon* and beg me to shaft her. Of course, my two roommates always pretended to be asleep. The doctor should have kept his money. She was well past her use-by date, having been round the block more times than the ice cream man. I didn't envy these girls though, it must have been a demoralising way to earn a crust. Not that I was any better really. I was paid hourly to sit and talk shite. Only difference was that I didn't get my arse felt. Maybe I had the raw deal.

I came back to the *Gaijin* house from teaching one night. It was about seven in the evening and most of the hostesses had just woken up and begun plastering their faces with make-up. Most of them slept all day and worked all night, and the layers of make-up were applied heavily to disguise the lack of sleep. There was a new addition to the *Gaijin* house, a *Cockney* whose name was Jimmy. He had just arrived from Thailand and looked a bit like a young *Tony Curtis*, with his deep brown suntan and flashing white teeth. The cocky bastard had his shirt off displaying a muscled torso, bulging biceps and a washboard stomach. He had a diamond stud in his ear and a golden *Buddha* dangling from a chain rested on his bulging hairless chest. He had colourful tattoos on each bicep; one was a *Union Jack* tied round the neck of a British bulldog and the other was a dagger with 'Death or Glory' written on it. He looked like a real powerhouse. Of course, the girls were all over him; fetching tea and biscuits, lighting his fags and gushing over his adventure stories.

I thought I was 'cock' of the *Gaijin* house but this smelt like competition and I didn't like the look of it! Jill would end up crawling into his *futon* if things carried on like this. He pulled out a harmonica and started playing. Not only was *Adonis* charming, he was also talented. I felt like sticking the harp up his arse and seeing if he could still play. I began to make myself a cup of tea and pottered around in the kitchen pretending not to listen to him.

He was telling a story about how hard it was to have a shit in India. I didn't catch the beginning but apparently he had been on crutches, so I took it he must have had a broken leg at the time. He said that the toilet had consisted of four concrete steps in the garden, which led nowhere. The idea was to climb the structure, then turn around and drop yir pants, get into a squatting position and poop from the top step. There was an abundance of local pigs whose staple diet was human shit. As soon as anyone made a move towards the steps the porkers would jostle each other for the best position to catch the flying turds. Due to the particular anthropological make up of these particular pigs, the weight of their heads prevented them from being able to point their little snouts skywards. Thus they were unable to anticipate the exact position of the flying dolphins as they were ejected from the landing bay. They could only hope in eager anticipation for a juicy brown trout to land nearby.

The benevolent Jimmy would choose the most deserving porker, activate the release button on his anal sphincter control pad and attempt to land the mother ship on the end of the designated piggy's snout. He said he imagined himself as the *Starship Enterprise* beaming down the Captain's Log. Although his aim improved dramatically over the course of a few days, a couple of obstacles arose which threatened to put an end to the target practice. Due to general poor hygiene in India, apparently one's bowel movements tend to liquefy with alarming haste. Another factor was the time element. If a man had to do what a man had to do he had best be quick off the mark, lest the crop spraying begin before he is in position.

Jimmy said the most horrifying moments were when he would suddenly awaken to the terrible realization that a number two was in the post, *express mail*. He would scramble on all fours out of the house, dragging his crutches behind him. He Reckoned the pigs must have posted sentries because he would immediately be surrounded by a ravenous pack of porkers. He knew he would never make the concrete outpost, not with the crutches, and anyway the *turtle's head* was already making its presence felt. He tried to squat but the greedy little buggers were lapping at his bum. He had no choice but to do his business whilst wriggling and sliding round the garden with his arse to the ground, beating off the pigs with his crutches. This being the only option, he left rather long snail tracks round the garden. This little circus was repeated at least three times a night, much to the delight of the pigs and the disgust of the other guests, who would wake up every day to a lawn that looked like the starting line at *Brands Hatch*. He interupted his reverie and addressed me.

"Oi mate. Pass us those will ya? All this talking about tom tit has made me wanna ave one."

He pointed behind me and I looked round to find a pair of crutches under my chair. As I passed them over to him he struggled to his feet and I noticed both his legs were skinny and deformed. I mumbled some apology.

"Sorry mate I didn't realise."

"Didn't realize wot! That I was a cripple! Is that wot you was gonna say? That you didn't realise I was a raspberry fucking ripple! I didn't realise you was a sweaty fuckin' sock but I ain't gonna hold it against ya."

I held out my mitt to shake his.

"My name's Dennis mate. Nice tae meet ya."

"Wotcha Den. I'm your new room mate, Jimmy. *Jocks* and cripples in room four. The two musketeers! I can't walk and you can't fuckin' talk!"

27

SKAGHEADS

LATER THAT NIGHT when Jimmy and I were alone in our room, I asked him if he had perhaps brought a little souvenir with him from Thailand. With a knowing grin he produced a small packet of white powder from his pocket.

"Is this wot you woz after Den? A bit of norty?"

We tore into the *heroin* like there was no tomorrow and in a very short space of time the cupboard was bare.

"Don't worry my old son, there's plenty more where that came from."

He produced a bigger, healthier looking packet from his pocket. *Heroin* is a great tongue loosener and it wasn't long before Jimmy filled me in on what he was really about. He had smuggled half a kilo of *smack* into Japan inside his amplifier. Reckoned he would get away with it once, this being his first trip to Japan, and had spent a couple of weeks on the beach in Thailand trying to get healthy for the trip. Bangkok is not an easy airport to leave unhindered if you are pasty-faced and pin-eyed.

Jimmy had been living in Thailand for the past year with a beautiful little stripper whose name was Toy, and he proudly showed me photographs of her. They had a kid together and Jimmy was doing this run so that she could stop stripping and they could buy a little cafe on the beach. They had been living in the worst slum in Bangkok, in an area called Klung Toy. He was really proud of his little boy and wanted a better life for him.

Jimmy told me about the night he had met Toy. After finishing her act she had sat down to have a drink with him, when this older French man came into the bar and started shouting at Toy and calling her a whore. The *Frog* grabbed her by the arm and slapped her so Jimmy picked up his crutch and hit the guy in the face with it. The bouncers at the club obligingly held the *Frog* down while Jimmy and Toy made a swift exit. Back at Toy's place in the slum she told Jimmy that the guy at the bar was actually her husband. He had taken her to live in Paris but she ran back to Thailand, leaving him because he was a very jealous and violent man. Jimmy had lived with Toy ever since. The pair of them had managed to survive on her earnings and whatever money Jimmy could make from selling drugs to tourists. But they couldn't carry on like that forever. He opened up his amp and brought out the half kilo.

"How much you reckon this is worth here Den?"

"Bundles!"

"Wanna make some money Den? Like I said, there's plenty more where this came from. I can have more sent if I find a market."

28

TEECHIR

JIMMY DIDN'T WANT the other residents to get suspicious, so he said he would keep busy by busking at nights, that way avoiding any awkward questions about how he earned his keep. He asked me if I knew any good spots to perform, so I arranged to meet him the next night after work at Shinjuku train station. I arrived to find him eyeing up every Japanese girl that walked past. It was refreshing to hear his Cockney banter so far from home.

"Phooawar! 'Ello luvverly. Oi, gis a smile."

I had been in Japan for a while now and was starting to feel like an ant. I was slowly becoming *Japanified*, walking around in cheap suits, polyester shirts and sensible shoes, talking mindless crap all day. Life in Japan does that to people after a while. It's like having a lobotomy. You begin to accept the *'Japanese way'* as reality, bowing and scraping and trying not to be noticed. Jimmy didn't give a toss who he upset with the great big amplifier strapped to his back. I felt like I had sold my soul for Japanese *Yen*, yet he retained his spontaneity, which is something most people have to sacrifice living in Japan.

Jimmy began his performance, playing blues on his harmonica to a taped accompaniment, going for the sympathy angle sitting down on the concrete with his crutches displayed against the amplifier for everyone to see. He was disabled, or *'shintie shogisan'* as they said in Japanese. He played for a couple of hours and made quite a bit of money. Then we went to the bar afterwards for a few drinks. I felt envious of his freedom to dress as he pleased and earn so much money from doing something he enjoyed; I really detested the daft English teacher's garb that I wore.

The Japanese are obsessed with the old collar and tie. It's one of those Western concepts of respectability and politeness that the Japanese have taken and made their own. Everyone in Japan wears a collar and tie, two pieces of cloth wrapped round their necks and pointing at their dicks.

There was one guy teaching at my school who was from one of those grim, cloth cap and whippet cities in the north of England. His name was Bill and he apparently had a black belt in *Ecki Thump*. Like me, Bill could see right through the bri-nylon troozirz and shirt and tie bollocks; it was all belt and braces where he came from. Bill was leaving Japan and the teaching profession. He had suffered it for a year and saved up enough money to go and live in some *real* Asian country for next to nowt on coconuts and *spliff*, and shag nut-brown native girls to your heart's content. After his final lesson Bill walked into the staff room and began to strip. Off came the tie, then the shirt and finally the bri-nylon troozirz. Then he took off his smart but sensible shoes and dumped all of the offending articles in the bin. Bill stood there in his Y-fronts, fists clenched in the air with a look of sheer bliss on his face. I don't think our Japanese colleagues could quite grasp the message being put across here, but I knew exactly where he was coming from. The only people who wore ties round my manor were detectives, and you wouldn't want to be seen talking to them now would you?

There I was, a hard-working English teacher with my specialised curriculum which included *Hang Man*, colouring pencils and *join the dots*; waking up bright and early every morning to attend to my serious language studies, diligent student that I was, and here was this chancer Jimmy blowing a few tunes of an evening on the street and making ten times the dosh I was making. Something wasn't quite right. It niggled me to think of all the effort I put into my education; years of hard graft to obtain my MAs, BAs, PhDs and Doctoral Thesis, and this scruffy piss-taker strolls through the back door to steal the goose that laid the golden egg!

I was back in the remedial class now after my exam escapade but I didn't mind starting from scratch. My language skills were steadily improving, but not because of my classroom application. It was due more to the number of Japanese girlfriends I had. There was no shortage of girlie students wanting *private lessons* from the teacher. Most of the girls joined English schools in the hope of romance with one or more of the teachers. Sure there is the public facade of colouring books and joining dots, but it's after the bell rings and the books are closed that the harmonious intermingling of foreign cultures really begins. In Japan it is quite common to see the nerdiest bespectacled Western geeks with really cute Japanese girls. These sad looking nerds would never pull anything of that calibre in their own countries, but believe it or not, to the Japanese, we *Gaijin* all look the same. Therefore, it didn't matter if you looked like *Brad Pitt* or *Herman Munster*, you could still pull a girl in Japan. My new Japanese language teacher was male so things were easier in the classroom. He realized that my only reason for attending school was to get a student visa, so he didn't bother trying to teach me anything.

I had a part time job teaching in a Japanese high school. The head teacher warned me on the first day that this was a very tough school with a reputation for bad behaviour, and that I should be very careful of troublemakers. But compared to where I went to school in Scotland these kids were angels. Of course, a few of the young thugs would get lippy now and again but this was done within the bounds of humour. It was the young girls who were the nightmare. They would sit there with their little mirrors applying lipstick and mascara. Any reprimand from me was met with such a barrage of abuse I decided to leave them alone. These girls would tell me that I was the smelliest foreign piece of shit ever shat into existence and that I should piss off back to my own country. Shocking behaviour! In my first ever lesson there were about seventy mixed-sex students in the classroom, all aged about sixteen.

Before-hand in the staff room, the teachers had instructed me not to speak Japanese under any circumstances, because if the students realised I could understand Japanese they wouldn't bother trying to speak English. I decided to play along if it was going to help the kids learn. A teacher led me into the classroom, introduced me to the students and instructed them to ask me some questions in English. A short tough looking kid asked the first question. He asked me how long I had been in Japan. I answered slowly and deliberately.

"I have been in Japan for seven months now."

"Can you speak Japanese?"

"I don't understand any Japanese. Not one word."

He then spoke to the class in Japanese and roughly translated he said,

"What kind of fuckin idiot are you? Been here seven months and you can't speak one word? That makes you rather more stupid than we could ever hope to be!"

I fell about laughing while the Japanese teacher reprimanded him for being cheeky. They knew I could at least understand the lingo and we spent many happy hours playing *Hang Man* after that.

29

YACHI-TACHI

I LIKED TO rush home after work and get out of the clown suit, then go up and meet Jimmy playing in Shinjuku. Sometimes when the crowds got too big, he would get hassled by the cops and told to move along. The cops are like everyone else in Japan, extremely polite. There wouldn't be any rough stuff, just a polite request to move along. Sometimes the Yakuza or Japanese mafia would demand a monthly fee for playing in their area. It wasn't much, maybe fifty dollars for the month. Protection Money.

Even the *mafia* were polite. A guy would come up and bow, give you his business card and introduce himself as a member of one of the *mafia* organisations. These low-ranking message boys were called '*chimpira*' and their job was to go around collecting protection money from the local businesses including street performers.

There is a uniformity of dress in Japan for almost every section of society. The way you dress expresses what you are, be it businessman, punk, rockabilly, high school student, or *Yakuza*. The *Yakuza* are easily identifiable by their tightly curled hair. This is known as a 'punch perm', and is done with curling tongs. The style is *de-rigueur* for Japanese gangsters. The other pointers are white shoes and missing pinkies, sometimes from both hands. (They chop these off themselves in a ceremony to apologise to the boss for a mistake. The severed fingers are then pickled and kept behind the boss's desk in jars.)

Most of the *Yaks* drive *Mercedes* or *BMWs* with dark windows, which are apparently illegal in Japan. There was a *Yakuza* office in Shinjuku on the main street. All these flash cars with dark windows coming and going, and these curly-haired, white-shod, pinkie-less tough guys standing around outside. Someone left the door open once and I got a look inside while I was walking past. There was a big fish tank inside with piranhas in it. Maybe that's where the pinkies ended up!

Jimmy had business cards provided by the *Yaks*, and would produce one of these for inspection if anyone else came to demand money. Even the cops were afraid of the *Yaks*. I saw one *Yak* park his Mercedes really badly, leaving a big gap from the curb. The cop politely asked the *Yak* to move his car, to which the *Yak* responded by punching the cop in the gob, then walking casually into his office. Japan doesn't really have a lot of street crime. The act of taking out societal beefs on inanimate objects such as bus shelters and parked cars isn't very popular with sons of Nippon. There is an expression that says policeman have two pairs of shoes - one wooden pair and one straw, indicating that police sometimes don the footwear of the gangsters. It's a very old expression, and I don't think the cops wear wooden shoes anymore than the *Yakuza* wear straw sandals, but the expression demonstrates that the *Yakuza* are a very powerful organisation deeply engrained in Japanese society, and that they have the law in their pocket. They even have their own representatives in parliament. In other societies it's wise to conceal your criminal activities. Here they wear it like a badge.

The *Yaks* were all involved in *Mizu-showbaii* which means *water business*, but in reality involves the seamy realms of *Karaoke* bars, alcohol, prostitution and drugs.

The most popular drug in Japan was *shabu-shabu*. Pure crystal methamphetamine. In the West it's called *speed* or *ice*. Japanese society demands people work long and hard so this drug is widely used by all kinds of people. Businessmen, students, hostesses, taxi drivers!. It's easily obtainable. Just ring up the *Yakuza* for a home delivery.

Me and Jimmy went to a Japanese *reggae* club one night. There were a few black guys there, the rest of the crowd were Japanese dressed up like Jamaican *rastas*. They had perfected the look. The clothes, the dreadlocks; they even danced like black men. But what cracked me up were their feet. Japanese people have small feet and black men have big feet. So these wannabe *rastas* had on two pairs of shoes; one inside the other one to make their feet look bigger than they actually were.

One Saturday night there was a bit of hassle in Shinju-kui. Jimmy had a huge crowd around him; most of them were drunken Japanese salary men. Poor bastards! The ultimate in wage slaves, no wonder they got legless. Anyway, the cops came along because the crowd was too big and too rowdy. The police hadn't seen Jimmy's crutches against the amplifier but the crowd had. The crowd were egging Jimmy on and throwing money at him, so Jimmy would blow a few more notes on the harmonica to wind up the *old bill*. It is very un-Japanese to argue against authority and all the salarymen's pent up frustrations started spilling out. They were just having a laugh. Jimmy wasn't really doing any harm so why couldn't the cops just let him play?

The cops demanded that the crowd stop throwing money in Jimmy's hat. It was just one of these situations where these people were probably so sick of being told what to do, and now that they had the Dutch courage, they decided to rebel against authority and started to empty their pockets into Jimmy's hat. The cops were screaming at them to stop, at the same time grabbing Jimmy by the shoulders. Of course, they were completely unaware that it was impossible for Jimmy to stand up without his crutches, something he was trying hopelessly to point out to them. A couple of cops managed to get Jimmy halfway up from the ground, then his legs started to wobble. It was evident they thought he was taking the piss, as they started poking his legs with their night sticks to make him stand up straight. All these salary men started calling the police all kinds of names and continued to throw their dosh into Jimmy's hat. I thought about intervening but it was too funny. Anyway, Jimmy was making some serious coinage so he wouldn't have thanked me. The cops ended up dragging some of the salary men off to the cooler!

30

RUNNERS

JIMMY TOLD ME that a couple of his mates were arriving next day from Bangkok, and asked if I would go with him to meet them at Ueno Station. We went the next afternoon and waited outside the station.

"Where are your mates from?"

"I don't know."

"Well, what do they look like?"

"I don't know."

"Well, if you don't know what they look like or where they're from, how can they be your mates then?"

A couple of straggly looking white guys came through the gates. One of them had a shaved head and the other one had teeth like gravestones.

"You Jimmy?"

Jimmy nodded and they followed us to a taxi. One of them was complaining of stomach cramps and said he had to hurry up and get to a toilet. I suggested using the one in McDonalds but they all looked at me like I was an idiot. We took a cab to some crummy hotel.

Jimmy booked two rooms and we went upstairs with them. The bald one ran straight to the bog, and you could hear him grunting away like he was giving birth. It turned out the guys were drug couriers. Jimmy had arranged with a partner in Bangkok to send these guys up to Japan on a run. Baldy had swallowed 450 grams of *heroin*, the other nearly a kilo of *hash*. The guy in the toilet comes out and hands us a handful of pellets then goes back inside and starts grunting again. Jimmy carefully cuts open a pellet with a knife and makes a few lines with the white powder.

We started getting stuck into the *smack*, smoking it and sniffing it. I felt great but I had to throw up. That's the strange thing about *heroin*; everything is enjoyable, even chucking your guts up. I made a beeline for the bog that Baldy had occupied. He had a couple of newspapers on the floor and was plopping out pellets in his shit. I threw up in the unused toilet. When I went back into the room where other guy was starting to complain of stomach pains. Jimmy tells him to leave off the *smack* or he won't be able to shit. At the same time he pockets a few pellets, giving the guy some *Yen* and telling them we will be back in the morning after the runners had shed their loads.

In the taxi back to the *Gaijin* house, Jimmy started to educate me. He could get kilos of *hash* and *smack* flown in from Bangkok. *Smack* in Japan at that time was worth anything between three and five hundred US dollars a gram. The Japanese weren't used to pure *gear*, so we could stamp all over it using glucose and vitamin powder. This move was obviously profit orientated, but we figured we were actually doing the *junkies* a favour. On one hand we reduced the chances of overdose, and on the other, we made sure they got a daily dose of vitamins. The profit percentage was high. Higher than teaching *Hang Man* or joining the dots, that's for sure!

Jimmy said he had two runners a week coming from Thailand. He also had people sending him *acid* from Europe. Sometimes the runners had swallowed *smack*, sometimes *hash* or even Thai *grass* pellets. The problem with the *grass* was it was too bulky, and the runners couldn't swallow as much, but a lot of the Japanese would pay fortunes for good Thai *grass* when they got sick of smoking *hash*. The only drug that could be labelled as 'Made in Nippon' was *shabu-shabu*, and that stuff made people all speedy and edgy. They were glad to get something decent to bring them down.

Jimmy offered me a full time position with his firm and the money was just too good to turn down. I gave up the teaching job and the language study and started going out to clubs more, looking for new drug customers. Most of the time I had to pick up the runners at Ueno station, take them to a cheap hotel, check them in, give them a couple of bob and tell them I would be back in the morning for the goods. Most of the runners were pretty clueless; generally skint *heroin* addicts hanging about in Bangkok without a make.

Asia is full of these long-term 'travellers' who end up penniless with no ticket, passport or visa. Some of them had just come out of Thai prisons, many of them with dodgy passports. Most of them had never been to Japan before, so we liked to keep them out of the way. We didn't want them asking too many questions and finding out how much money we were making. They were pretty desperate characters really, and sometimes got a bit big for their boots. I suppose that's why Jimmy wanted me in the firm really; heart of gold, nerves of steel and a knob of butter.

31

PUNX NOT DEAD

ONE MORNING I had to pick up a runner from Ueno Station. I spotted this guy with blonde spiky hair, wearing a leather biker's jacket and shirtless underneath the jacket. He was sitting on the stairs holding his stomach, moaning and groaning and reeking of booze. I motioned for him to follow me to a taxi.

Jimmy and I had rented a little room above a shop near the *Gaijin* house. I had told the old woman, Keiko, who owned the shop, that I was studying Japanese at the university and she let me have it cheap. She was a lovely old lady and would sometimes bring me pots of green tea or little cakes.

I showed up at the room where Jimmy was waiting with this *Billy Idol* look-alike. How *Billy Idol* got through customs dressed like that I have no idea. Jimmy rolled his eyes at him. *Billy* was moaning about being hungry so I took him to a noodle shop down the street, ordered him some food and waited outside

Japanese people are always looking at foreigners. Not impolitely or openly but they are always watching. *Billy Idol* was far too loud in his dress and manner so I didn't really want to be seen with him. I could see him gesturing and waving in the noodle shop, sending his noodles back, as he didn't like them. Then he ordered a beer. I waited till he drank the beer then went in to drag him out, which wasn't easy as he had decided he wanted more beer. I stamped on his feet under the table and twisted his arm a bit as I dragged him out the door, all the while smiling at the staff and pretending it was a joke. The other customers loved this spectacle. After all it wasn't everyday *Billy Idol* comes into their local noodle shop shirtless and pissed.

Maybe I was being a bit hard on this guy, but the longer one stays in Japan the more self conscious one becomes. Any outward signs of emotion embarrass the Japanese, therefore the public face must remain calm and serene. The longer I was there, the more I would cringe at the way some Westerners conducted themselves in public. *Billy Idol* was pissing me off, so I manhandled him out of the shop which was almost across from the stairs leading to our apartment. We were just about to go upstairs when he decided he had to get razor blades from Keiko-san's shop. I tried to pull him by the arm but old Keiko-san was looking out of the shop window smiling at us, so I smiled back and let him go. He went staggering into the shop and seemed to be taking forever; picking things up, inspecting them, and then putting them down again. I was losing my patience so I went into the shop and snarled at him to hurry up. Keiko-san bowed and smiled at me. I got him out of the shop and upstairs into the room. As soon as we got there I started telling Jimmy what a complete arsehole this guy was. *Billy Idol* then produced a packet of razor blades from his inside pocket and goes,

"Oi! Look wot I just nicked!"

I gave him sharp backhand slap, knocking him to the floor. Jimmy had to restrain me from jumping up and down on him, because this piece of shite was carrying precious cargo. What kind of arsehole goes shoplifting with half a kilo of *skag* in his stomach? Eventually he fell asleep, which we were glad of because we were both sick and tired of him by now. Whilst *Billy* was sleeping it off, me and Jimmy decided to go out. When we came back, we found *Billy* curled up under a blanket, his jeans and leather jacket lying beside him. There didn't seem to be any sign of the precious little packages. Things were getting a wee bit desperate here. Jimmy was showing signs of withdrawal, having spent many years cultivating his habit. I had always thought the oncoming signs of *cold turkey* were in his head. I didn't believe in alcoholism or addiction at that time but that was about to change.

Jimmy decided to call a friend for some advice.

"Hello mate! Its Jimmy here. A friend of mine seems to be having difficulty with a bowel movement, or should I say lack of movement. What's that? *Spliff* helps does it?"

Jimmy kicked the sleeping beauty out of his blanket, sticking a *joint* in his face.

"Oi you! Smoke this!"

Billy Idol was struggling to get his bearings. He took the *joint* and started puffing on it. I don't think he even knew what planet he was on. He was scrutinising us like he had never seen us before, and to top it all, he was wearing, believe it or not, a shiny silver thong! A little ball bag and a sliver of string that disappeared up the crack of his scrawny little hairy arse. Poor bastard! Standing there like a frightened animal with ribs like a toast rack and us falling about laughing at him. We fed him laxatives with some food and eventually he jumped up and declared he was now ready to curl one. Jimmy was especially delighted because mild *heroin* withdrawals had already started. Shakes and sniffles. There was a little shower area sectioned off from the rest of the room by a plastic shower curtain. *Thrilly Knickers* went behind the screen to shed his load.

We sat down in front of the TV when there was a knock at the door. I went to open it and it was old Keiko-san with some green tea on a tray and some little cakes on it. I tried to take the tray off her but she bowed politely and assured me it was OK, she could carry it inside herself. Maybe she had noticed that *Thrilly Knickers* had stolen razor blades from her shop and wanted to get a better good look at him. She walked past me and put the tray down, then started to pour the tea for us asking, "Shimpatsu no hito wa?" Meaning, "Where is Blondie?." I smiled and nodded toward the curtain area and said, "Ofuro des."

Japanese are obsessive about personal hygiene, so she seemed pleased with the answer. I had said he was having a bath. *Thrilly Knickers* starts to grunt.

"Oooooaaaaar! Ooooooaaaaah! Oh fuck, ny arse looks like a Japanese flag! Ooo yii bastard ooooo ya cuntya ! Aahh... One out!"

There was a plopping sound followed by a loud fart.

"That's one load. Do you want it now?"

I took a sip of tea and picked up a cake.

"Oish so, conno cakie, des nae Keiko-San. These cakes look delicious, Mrs Keiko."

The smell of the shit is almost unbearable. Mr *Thrilly Knickers* is obviously delighted with himself.

"Oooaaahhh! Fuck me gently, whoa ya bastard ya, my fuckin arsehole is like a blood orange! Two out!" Plop, fart.

Jimmy started to snigger first. I choked on my cake trying to hold back a fit of uncontrollable giggles. Keiko-san left. *Confucius, he say: Man who laughs last doesn't get joke.*

32

JIMMY TRAVOLTA

I HAD BEEN caning a lot of smack to combat the coke and speed. My pockets were full of every drug under the sun and I would get stuck into all of them at once. One of my favourites were these really good colourful window acid tabs, and Tokyo is a great place for a trip. I would neck two or three trips and go and do my laundry. Sit there watching the clothes go round. Or go to the traditional bathhouse and sit in the hot bath with a load of old Japanese men with towels on their heads singing traditional Japanese folk songs.

One night me and Jimmy went out to a club. The *no dancing* law had been done away with by now, so there were quite a few discos. Me and Jimmy had gone into the club's toilet to sniff some *coke*. Jimmy couldn't hold his drink or his drugs, so it was always up to me to accompany him to the toilet for a sniff. Other people could nip in and out the bogs, but this wasn't so easy with Jimmy and his crutches. Drink and drugs didn't really mix well with his disability. Straight and sober he was a diamond, but when he got out of it his complexes would come out and he would start fights or grab girls' arses.

It was on one such night in the club that me and Jimmy staggered off to the karzee for a toot of *Charlie*. Jimmy was like a ravenous dog as he watched me open my wallet and fish out the packet. It wasn't until I opened the wrap that I realised that it wasn't *coke* after all, it was *smack*. Jimmy started to burn the paper off the tinfoil in his cigarettes and he held the fort while muggins ran back to get the *coke* from my fag packet on the table. Being a bit out of it, I had made the stupid mistake of leaving my wallet in the bog with Jimmy. Upon my return, I found that the bold Jimmy had smoked his way through half of the *heroin* and rifled through my wallet.

"C'mon Jimmy give them back."

"Give what back?"

"The *dragons* man! I had blotting paper in there, eight *trips*."

"Eight?"

"Yes! Eight."

"I thought it was two. There were only two *dragons*."

"Yes! But each picture of a dragon has four detachable pieces, Jimmy. Hence, eight *trips*!"

"I've eaten them!"

"You've eaten eight *trips*?"

"Yes, I thought it was two. I could handle two!"

"I wouldn't like to be in your shoes mate! It'll be a straight jacket and a fucking padded cell with rubber cutlery for you!"

We went back to the table and sat down. The first sign that Jimmy was losing the plot was when he tried to order drinks from the waiter. He was making hand signals but couldn't articulate. He was having problems counting up to two and couldn't decide how many fingers indicated two drinks, so he tried with his other hand. The waiter gave up and walked away.

The music was early house disco and the DJ increased the tempo. Jimmy started making these mad hand signals and decided to cut the carpet. He shuffled off towards the dance floor with his head bobbing in time with the music. Jimmy had never really been one for the dancing. Maybe it was the trip I had taken earlier, but with the rapid jerky movements and the strobe light, Jimmy looked remarkably like a good break-dancer. The backward moonwalk was a disaster though, and he fell flat on his arse. He was up on his feet sharp though, bobbing and jerking like a mad man. Not surprisingly the other people on the dance floor gave him a wide berth. He pulled the harmonica out of his pocket and started blowing into it as he danced. Jimmy's movements got wilder. He grabbed an umbrella from behind the DJ box and put it up on the dance floor. Blowing into his harmonica, twirling the brolly above his head, trying to moonwalk like Michael Jackson, he then decided to get his gear off. First the jacket, followed by the shirt, then the trousers. He was in his undies and the dance floor had cleared. The manager signalled to the DJ and the music was switched off.

"Switch the fucking music back on you Japanese bastard!"

Jimmy was using the umbrella like a sword and he lunged towards the DJ, sticking the point of the umbrella up his nose. The manager came up and asked me to get my friend out or he would have no alternative but to call the police. Luckily, there was a lift to fling him into; I couldn't have imagined getting him down any stairs. Getting him in a headlock, I dragged him kicking and screaming into the lift.

"I wanna fucking dance! That's all I want! To fucking dance! Let me dance you bastard, let me dance!"

The manager handed me Jimmy's clothes and I managed to get him dressed. Getting a taxi proved difficult as nobody wanted him in their cab. I went for the sympathy angle and waved Jimmy's crutches at all the passing cars 'til eventually one taxi driver felt sorry for us and gave us a ride. Back home, I had to pour half a bottle of *Valium* down his neck just to shut him up.

33

INTO THE HABIT

A COUPLE OF Jimmy's runners had got busted at the airport in Japan, so we had to lay low for a bit. We rented this shitty little room somewhere in a place called Shin-Okubo.

We were getting low on *smack* and Jimmy was worried about getting sick. I had never experienced *cold turkey* before and didn't really believe in alcoholism or drug addiction. On the odd occasions we had run out of *smack*, Jimmy would lay on his bed for days, shivering, shaking and puking. I might have felt a bit shivery but refused to entertain it, so would drop another couple of *trips*, smoke some *speed*, and go out to a club. Once I got a few whiskeys down my neck, I would be fine.

This time, I left Jimmy to his misery and went out on a mission. As luck would have it I managed to procure some *gear* from some dodgy Indian blokes I had met the week before.

I returned to the room to find Jimmy huddled up on his *futon* and surrounded by an assortment of painkillers, sleeping tablets and tissues; all the necessary ingredients to get through the *turkey*.

"Are you asleep?"

"Fuck off!"

"Would you like a nice cup of tea Jimmy?"

"Fuck off!"

He was whimpering like a little puppy. His legs were shaking like jelly. That's probably why they call it *kicking the habit!* The body produces natural painkillers called *endorphins*, but if you take the *heroin* for long enough, the body stops producing natural painkillers as the *heroin* gives you ample protection against pain.

To be *stoned* on *heroin* is to be totally relaxed in a cocoon of physical and mental relaxation and well-being. It's like being back in the womb. Take away the *heroin* and your body is incapable of producing the natural substances that make it physically comfortable to make contact with other objects, like sitting on a chair or lying on a bed. Take this to a psychological level and it is very uncomfortable just to 'be' any other way but *stoned*. That is when reliance happens. Your body sends messages to your brain telling it that things are not as they should be. Physical dependence in itself is strong enough, but your brain remembers how nice it was in that cocoon and wants to go back there. Real life just doesn't cut it anymore.

"Jimmy, try some of this. It might make you feel better."

"Fuck off!"

I put a bit of *gear* on some tinfoil and started smoking it. Within seconds Jimmy recognised the smell. Talk about greased lightning; you have never seen anyone move so quickly. Doctors have done tests showing that the adrenalin rush is actually higher when you procure a drug, rather than when you use it. It was certainly true in Jimmy's case.

He was out of his *futon* like a shot, consuming as much as humanly possibly in the shortest amount of time imaginable. We phoned up the Indian bloke and ended up buying a couple of hundred grams from him. I started to really cane the *smack*, doing more and more. People say you have to keep increasing the amounts to get *stoned*. This wasn't the case with me; I just couldn't get anymore *stoned*. I don't know what come over me. For about two weeks I just lay there and got stuck into it, smoking so much foil my throat was killing me. I was coughing up all sorts of horrible black phlegm, resulting in my throat being inflamed and swollen. I had to stop smoking the smack, not because I wanted to stop, but it was just that my poor throat couldn't handle the burning tinfoil taste anymore. I suppose I could have sniffed it but I still hadn't realised how hooked I was. Not understanding what was happening to me, I put the cause of my illness down to the chemicals in the foil. It just didn't occur to me that I was about to experience my first symptoms of *heroin* withdrawal.

I just wanted to hide my head away and felt this obsession to bury my head somewhere, a bit like an ostrich really. I started to shake and shiver and couldn't keep still. I lay there just whimpering and vomiting for about four days. The whole time I had been sick, I never had the sense to realise that it was the *smack*. If it had occurred to me earlier that a little *toot* would have taken away my sickness, then *toot* I would have. Jimmy was sitting on his *futon* smoking *gear*.

"C'mon, mate. Have a go on this. It'll make you feel much better!"

Jimmy handed me the foil. I took the stuff from him even though I knew what it would do to me. I couldn't help myself. I was depressed and wanting to get back into the comfort zone. From then on I couldn't last a day without *smack*. That experience brought about a fundamental change in my personality.

Up until then, whenever things in my life didn't go the way I wanted them to, I would go and have a few drinks and forget about it. I'd always been a reckless gung-ho survivor. Now, life became a constant search for *smack*. If I was running low, I would lie down and whimper like a sick child, becoming a complete wimp without my supply of *smack*.

What I couldn't work out was, if I already knew from my first *turkey* how powerfully addictive the stuff was, then why on earth would I pick it up again? There was no logic in it! Where was my reasoning, my intellect, and my natural human instinct to protect myself from what is harmful? Sure, ants eat themselves to death in the sugar but I wasn't a fucking ant! You didn't have to be Albert Einstein to know that *smack* was bad for you. Jimmy told me about a medical experiment in the States that he had seen on TV. The experiment was done on humans and chimpanzees to monitor the behaviourial patterns and distinguish the different attitudes (if any) between man and animals towards addiction. The human contingent consisted of volunteer *heroin* addicts who agreed to take free *heroin* for one month. Then when they had a full-fledged habit going, the supply was to be stopped suddenly, with no medicines to ease the withdrawal symptoms. There was no shortage of human *guinea pigs*. The apes on the other hand had no choice. In the first few days the *junkies* would stick their arms out to receive the injections but the apes had to be forced. After a few days the apes got into the swing of things, so to speak, volunteering their arms through the bars of their cages to receive the *smack*. A happy month was spent by all in the *heroin* comfort zone!

When the supply stopped, the humans knew what to expect and lay down and accepted the inevitable sickness. The apes didn't know what was going on and showed their up-turned arms through the bars for the expected dosage. When no *smack* was forthcoming, the apes became angrier and angrier. The poor apes had a horrible four days of *cold turkey*, not understanding any of it. *Cold turkey* seemed to affect both apes and humans in the same way; hot and cold sweats, diarrhoea, vomiting, and whimpering. On the fifth day, people were beginning to perk up again, and everyone seemed to be through the ordeal. The addiction was over, at least in the physical sense. Their bodies were no longer physically dependent on heroin. But the physical symptoms, although painful, are not the real problem. Getting over the physical addiction is nothing compared to the mental longing.

The addicts were again offered heroin. Even though they knew they didn't need it and that they would be sick again, all of them came forward one by one for a fix. The apes refused. The doctors tried to force the apes into taking an injection, but the apes fought so violently it was impossible to inject them. They would rather be killed than have to take this stuff inside their bodies again. Animals know by instinct alone what is good for them.

The *junkies* decided that *cold turkey* was bad, but it was worth it. The animals' basic instinct assured them that it wasn't. We think of animals as lesser beings, but if it were my ability to reason that makes me a *junkie*, I would rather do without it.

34

KICKBOXER

OUR JAPANESE VISAS were running out, so Jimmy suggested a trip to Thailand. He was missing his wife and kid, worrying because he hadn't heard from her for a while. I had never been to Thailand, and reckoned I needed a break from the monotony of the concrete metropolis. We both wanted to break our skag habits, so perhaps Thailand wasn't the ideal place to try and come off the gear. Jimmy wanted to try and clean up a bit before meeting his missus. He didn't want her or the kid to see him in such a state. The pair of us flew to Bangkok where we stayed in Sukumvit to get away from the backpack and Birkenstock brigade in Kaosan Road.

A hospital that deals with drug addicts in Bangkok gave us some *methadone* to ease us off the *smack*. We caught an internal flight to the island of Koh Samui, taking the *methadone* with us. Managing to reduce my dosage every day, within a week I was off the *smack* and the *methadone*, but had started smoking *spliff* obsessively.

Jimmy and I had adjoining bungalows on the beach. I started doing a bit of training; swimming, running, and getting healthy. We travelled round the adjoining islands a bit, checking out the scenery. The owner of the bungalows we stayed at had been a professional *Muay Thai Kickboxer*, and he had a little boxing stable near the kitchen with punch-bags, ropes, pads and other boxing kit. I was starting to get fit and healthy and a bit of sun always does wonders to make one look and feel better. Some of the kids at the gym were pretty good, but their punching techniques needed some work. I taught them how to punch better, but no way would I ever learn how to kick as hard as them. They had legs like concrete and kicked like mules.

Some of the boys were fighting one night at a show in town, and me and Jimmy decided to go along to watch. The boxing was held in this large pub-club place, and it was packed with both Thais and foreigners. We had acquired front row seats, squeezed in alongside this scraggly ginger-bearded Australian guy. He had his arm round this little Thai prostitute who couldn't have been more than sixteen years old. Catching me looking at her, he expressed his feeling for her as only an Australian could.

"What d'ya reckon cobber? Pretty spunky eh? You know what I'm gonna do with her when I get her home? I'm gonna drink her bathwater, then I'll suck her shit to a point. Then I'm gonna lick her from head to foot and start all over again."

The first thing we watched was a snake show that was performed inside the boxing ring. First of all the snake man would prove that his snakes were the real thing by demonstrating milking the fangs of a poisonous snake. This he did by covering the top of a drinking glass with cling-film and causing the snake sink his fangs into it. The poison could be seen dripping into the glass. Unwilling volunteers were grabbed and pulled into the ring where snakes were then wrapped round their necks or even put down their trousers. The snake-man pretended to fling snakes into the crowd, scattering everyone. A glass case about one meter square was then put into the middle of the ring. Into this was dropped a cobra and a cover put quickly over it. The cobra was standing up in the cage, hooded and deadly. Music from *Chariots of Fire* then started playing and the presenter got on the microphone.

"Ladies and gentlemen! The challenger! The number one contender for the crown! The undefeated. The undisputed *Marvellous Marvin, the mongoose!*"

The crowd went wild as this bloke came out of the dressing room with a jet-black mongoose on a lead. The mongoose was so cute, complete with a little pink fluffy collar with a bell. It was sniffing at peoples' feet as it went up to the ring and everybody was patting it. The presenter held it up in the centre of the ring and the little chap started licking his face. Betting got underway for the contest between *Marvellous* the mongoose, and the deadly poisonous cobra. The drum roll commenced, the betting was fast and furious, and the presenter opened the glass top while another guy pushed an eager *Marvellous Marvin* inside.

Marvin was crouched in the middle of the cage looking at the cobra. The cobra wasn't even looking at *Marvin*. He was looking out of the glass case towards the crowd. I asked a Thai man sitting behind me why the snake didn't seem interested.

"The snake no want to looking in mongoose eyes. Snake only attack if look in its eye. Mongoose know this. He challenge snake. When their eyes meet, they will fight and mongoose kill him."

"How do you know the mongoose will win?"

"Because *Marvellous Marvin*! He always kill snake."

I bet a few quid on *Marvin*. Jimmy put his money on the snake. Marvin edged closer to the snake. The snake pushed his face against the glass. *Marvin* was pushing his own face against the glass trying to make eye contact with the snake; sort of like looking over the snake's shoulder, only snakes don't have shoulders.

Marvin was giving it the big one, doing his best to make the snake meet his gaze, his eyes moving from one side of the snake's head to the other, but the snake was completely blanking him. Suddenly their eyes met and it kicked off. Snake and mongoose were writhing around the glass cage wrapped around each other. Within a few short seconds the snake is lying lifeless in the bottom of the cage and *Marvin* was tearing great lumps out of it. The presenter took the case top off and held a triumphant *Marvin* up with one hand, the dead snake with the other.

The presenter asked the crowd if they wanted more and the crowd went wild. One of the Thais pulled another cobra out of a sack; a bigger, fatter one this time. Everyone roared their approval. He demonstrated the poison in the fangs again by milking a tiny bit of venom into a glass. *Marvin* didn't look at all concerned. The nonchalant look on his furry little face clearly expressed that he had seen it all before. The Thai pulls another fat cobra out of the sack. Two cobras! This made *Marvin* perk up. The betting went mad. The cobra brothers were even favourites with poor old *Marvin* trailing at 9 to 1. Jimmy doubled his bet. To be honest I was about to bet on the cobra brothers myself as I didn't fancy *Marvin's* chances, but as I turned around, I caught the eye of the little Thai prostitute with the *Aussie* and she mouths "*Marvin*."

I mouthed the word back again to make sure.

"*Marvin*," she nodded and mouthed back, so I put my money on the mongoose. Both snakes were looking out towards the crowd. *Marvin* was poised, crouched in the middle of the case looking from snake to snake. Neither of the snakes wanted to know as *Marvin* was taunting them with the evil eye. Eventually one of the snakes had no choice. With *Marvin* breathing down his neck, the cobra turns around, and off it goes. It was too fast to see what went on, but *Marvin* and the cobra brothers really went for it. Inside a minute both snakes were dead and *Marvin* was lifted victorious to the roar of the crowd.

The snake shows cleared off and there was an interval before the *Thai Boxing* commenced. Before the boxers started fighting, they did a little ritual dance in apology to the gods for striking each other with the lowest, dirtiest part of their bodies, the feet.

Thai Boxing is notoriously lethal; just about anything goes apart from head-butting and kicking in the bollocks. Most of the bouts ended with one of the opponents unconscious and carried from the ring. It was pretty gruesome stuff. Knees to the face, elbows to the temple or solar plexus! There were about ten bouts in all. After the last fight, a boxer got into the ring alone and the presenter asked if anyone wanted to challenge him. The prize money was one hundred US Dollars. The fighter was walking around the ring challenging different people in the audience to fight. Jimmy is pointing at me, shouting,

"He'll have you mate! He'll have you!"

The presenter walks towards me and speaks into the microphone asking, "Do we have a challenger?" The presenter was taunting me, along with the fighter.

"Are you scared? Are you man enough?"

There was no way on earth I was getting in that ring. The fighter looking pretty fearsome, and anyway, I had been drinking all night. The whole audience was clapping and egging me on thanks to Jimmy. The *Aussie* next to me started winding me up.

"C'mon yi pommie bastard! What's a matter with you? Fucking scared?"

"Yes thank you *Bruce*. I'm scared"

"Fucking poofter."

Bruce's little girlfriend was shaking her head at me telling me not to do it. I don't mind a challenge but this wasn't sport, this was lethal. Then suddenly *Bruce* jumped up and tore off his T-shirt.

"C'mon ya Thai bastard! I'll fucking have you!"

His girlfriend was seriously against the idea, but he was drunk. The crowd was egging him on, and he went off to the changing room to get gloved up. Everyone was going completely mental now that they had their sacrificial lamb. His little girlfriend looked terrified. I felt truly sorry for her. These *Thai Kickboxers* train from childhood hardening their legs. Foreigners cannot possibly hope to compete against the Thais. Their legs have been battered so hard, they usually die from cancer of the bone. This wasn't a boxing match. This was suicide.

Brucie came out wearing *Thai Boxing* shorts and gloves. He was a fit looking bloke, but he didn't know what he was getting into. The Thai went into this elaborate dance while the *Aussie* stood in the corner warming up. He was beginning to sober up pretty quickly; you could see the fear in his face. The referee brought the two fighters together in the centre of the ring to shake hands. There wasn't much difference in weight, but the Thai looked more solid and much, much meaner. The bell went and the Thai did a sweeping kick, which immediately brought the *Aussie* to his knees. The referee stepped in, helping him up. Brucie was looking a bit groggy when the Thai came at him again. He tried to hold on to the Thai by wrapping his arms around his neck. The Thai put his gloves behind *Brucie's* head and pushed his neck down hard, at the same time bringing up his knee into his face. It was such a powerful blow that the sound of his nose cracking could be heard quite clearly. The *Aussie* was carried unconscious and bleeding out of the ring. The Thai boxer walked over and started taunting me to come in next. The presenter was also egging me on. I stood up and shouted that I would fight him on one condition. That was we would box European style - no kicks, no elbows. It's not that I thought Thai boxers were any *harder* than normal boxers. I had seen bare knuckle fighting before between *kickboxers* and boxers where no-one threw any kicks.

The quickest and most effective way to knock someone out is a fist to the head. We would be wearing gloves here so my deadly weapons would be cushioned but his kicks wouldn't. The fighter agreed to box my way, European style. The crowd went mad, the betting increased, and I was led off to the changing room to get gloved up. I was sharing a dressing room with the snake-man and he watched me get ready whilst he played with his snakes. I stripped down to my jocks and was laid out on a bench in readiness for the two Thai boxers from my stable to massage my whole body with Thai lineament oil. It was extremely hot and made my breathing heavy.

The snake-man had a bag full of cobras which he opened to show me the snakes inside. Grimacing, I pulled my face away and he laughed. *Marvin* was asleep in his cage. Snake-man pulled a cobra out of the bag by its tail. It was big, fat and extremely angry. It started darting around the man's face. He stayed completely calm and avoided looking into the cobras eyes whilst still holding on to its tail. The cobra seemed satisfied that there was no challenge here and began to settle down. The cobra was then put on a table where it was sitting up erect and hissing. He slowly brought down his free hand, palm outstretched, and placed it over the cobras head, gently pushing the cobra down until it coiled up like it was asleep. The snake-man spoke to me.

"You want *spirit of snake*? Make you win fight."

Apparently cobra blood is a natural *steroid*; a lot of Asian fighters drink it before getting into the ring. I would need all the help I could get, so I agreed to drink the snake blood. To my horror and distaste, instead of putting the blood in a glass, snake-man insisted that the only way to get the *spirit of the snake* inside me was to suck it straight from the neck as soon as he had severed the head. He straightened out the cobra and with one fell swoop chopped its head off with a machete. I proceeded to suck the blood from the bleeding neck. The decapitated cobra was still wriggling and somehow managed to wrap itself round my hand, stopping the blood in my veins as I sucked the lifeblood from his.

Later when I shadow-boxed I could have sworn I saw a hood appearing round my neck. I looked in the mirror; my eyes looked reptilian and deadly. The guy cut the snake open and ripped out the beating heart. He told me to chew it at the same time telling me to lie back down on the massage table. It didn't taste too bad. Some powder was taken from a sack along with a long bamboo straw. He placed his fingers over my eyes and closed them as well as closing his own He prayed as he rubbed the powder between his hands, and then sucked the powder from within his cupped hands into his mouth. He placed the long bamboo straw inside my right nostril and blew the powdery contents of his mouth up inside my nose. It was wild, like one big speedy hallucinogenic cobra rush. I was a warrior going to battle, jogging up to the ring and leaping over the ropes.

The bell went and we met in the centre of the ring. I rushed him with a flurry of blows and pounded him into the corner. He brought his leg up and kicked me right in the balls. I was pole-axed, man, lying on the ground holding my nuts. The crowd started booing and chucking things into the ring, but instead of disqualifying my opponent the referee started counting me out. I managed to get to my feet but I was still in fucking agony. The referee gave us the signal to box and I put my guard up but the guy came under my guard with a kick and hit me in the stomach. There was only one way I was going to get any justice here. I put both hands up and signaled to stop. The crowd booed thinking I was bottling out.

I got hold of the laces of my left glove with my teeth and started to open the left glove. I pulled it off and then did the same thing with the right. The referee was waving his hands frantically trying to put a stop to it but the crowd loved it. My opponent followed suit and tore his gloves off with his teeth. He came towards me but I could smell the fear on him. *Kickboxer* ain't so cocky now! We stood toe to toe and exchanged blows.

I was stronger, heavier, and much angrier. I pounded him into the floor. The referee had to pull me off or I would have kept going. After the fight, I was in the changing room where people were slapping me on the back and congratulating me when my opponent staggered into the room. He had two black eyes, his nose was broken and some of his teeth were missing. I felt genuinely sorry for him. He had to do this for a living; I could always go back and get a McJob. He put his hand out and asked if I could give him some money for doctor. I had just won a hundred dollars of prize money and was making a move to pull some out when the other Thais got really angry and chased him out of the changing room.

"You beat him! You won money! You keep money!"

We went back to Jimmy's bungalow on the beach after the fight. After a few drinks and a few spliffs my body was still aching, so I decided to have a tiny miniscule little hit of *smack*. Just for the pain, mind. *Famous last words!*

Addiction is a progressive disease. I heard someone say once that addiction is always galloping alongside recovery. One taste and I was hooked again.

35

SCORING

WE WENT BACK to Bangkok and stayed in some shit-hole in Kaosan road, trying to blend in with the budget travellers with their Aqua bottles and beach mats. Why does every two-bob traveller carry a big bottle of water with him? Is there anywhere on the planet you can't buy water?

Jimmy showed up in the restaurant of the backpackers' fleapit hostel we were staying at. It was lunchtime and the restaurant was packed full of budget travellers. They were mostly gravitationally challenged, single, Germanic looking women, with underarms so hairy they looked like they had *Don King* in a headlock. Jimmy's idea was that we would try to blend in by staying in backpacker land. He came into the restaurant with a young prostitute who couldn't have been more than sixteen years old. She was wearing a mini-skirt and white high heels, a tinsel handbag draped over her shoulders. There is a time and a place for everything, but bringing an obvious young prostitute into a restaurant full of politically correct students wasn't exactly discreet, not in backpacker land. The place was full of plastic year-off hippies rabbiting on about rainforest depletion and the rape of the third-world by the market fundamentalism of the corporadoes... etc, etc.

The whole place turned round and stared, as Jimmy and his new girlfriend joined me at my table. This was typical of Jimmy. Anyone else would have paid the girl and sent her home in a taxi but Jimmy wanted to wind up a few wankers. I could hear numerous comments, "Outrageous", "Disgusting" and "Old enough to be her father," from the other tables.

"I thought we were supposed to blending in here Jim. Everybody's staring at us."

"Fuck them! They're only jealous."

Jimmy ordered some food then pulled out his wallet and made a big show of paying the girl. She grabbed the money and tottered out of the restaurant blowing kisses at everyone. Jimmy filled me in on the plan. We were to book our flights separately but for the same flight on *Egypt Air* from Bangkok to Tokyo. We would go and score the *smack* tonight. I asked him how the wife and kid were and he said he hadn't been to see them yet. He had been to the bar where she stripped, but they said she hadn't shown up at work for a couple of weeks. He said that the slum where he lived before with his missus was notorious for *smack,* and that it was dead easy to score there. Apparently, his wife's mother was one of the biggest dealers there, but we had better be careful leaving, because the cops had a tendency to follow foreigners leaving the slum. We would pack the stuff tonight, and tomorrow morning we would start swallowing. I asked Jimmy if it was a good idea to go to such a dodgy place to score.

"Look mate, I know! She has the strongest, purest *smack* in Bangkok. And it's cheap. If we try and score around here, we don't know who we're dealing with. We could end up either in jail or ripped off."

We went up to Jimmy's room for a few *schnorts,* and later on we got a cab to the slum. I was beginning to feel a bit shaky about the whole affair. I had a knife with me but most of the Thai crooks carry guns. I was the one elected to carry the cash of course, because I was supposed to be the tough guy. Jimmy kept nodding off in the taxi on the way to the slum. As usual, he had sniffed too much *smack* again and was dribbling all over his shirt. I had to keep shaking him awake.

"C'mon Jimmy, for fuck's sake get it together! I'm depending on you here. This is your gig man!"

Jimmy didn't seem too concerned. He treated everything as a big joke. The cab pulled up at the entrance of the slum and we got out. The sweat was pouring off Jimmy's brow as he dragged himself along on his crutches. We walked through a night market with stalls selling everything from electrical goods to underwear. We got through the market with the stink of greasy fried chicken and noodles sticking to our clothes, then onto a rickety bridge over a canal.

The slum was a maze of wooden or corrugated iron shacks built on stilts on top of the river. The stink of raw sewage and garbage was overwhelming. It was dark and there were shady looking characters appearing from the darkness.

"You want girl? You want *heroin*?"

Jimmy was our guide through the rickety bridges joining the shacks.

"It's a bit Abraham Lincoln isn't it?"

"What's that Jimmy?"

"Its pen and fucking inkin!"

Jimmy was your eternal cheeky, chirpy *Cockney*. All jellied eels and knees up Muvva Brahn.

"Cooah blimey! Me fucking plates are killing me and these fucking daisy roots are too small!"

"Jimmy will you shut your fucking trap and find the house."

Jimmy was off his nut and didn't really seem like he knew where he was going.

"I think it's this one."

Jimmy knocked on the door of a wooden shack. A young boy opened the door and Jimmy asked for Toy. The kid pointed Jimmy to another shack. We go and knock on this door but there is no answer. More and more slum residents were following us to see what we were up to. We were attracting far too much attention.

"When were you last here Jimmy?"

"About three months ago."

"Couldn't you have phoned first? Maybe she moved."

"They don't have telephones here you fuckin' pillark!"

There was a figure sleeping in a blanket beside the door so Jimmy prods him with his crutch.

"Oi! Arfur!"

The bundle of rags gets up sleepily and looks at us through half closed eyes.

"Jimmy?"

Then he smiled this big toothless grin at us, opened the door of the shack and invited us in. We sat down and Jimmy asked Arfur where Toy is.

"France. She go back with husband."

Jimmy looked devastated. He asked when she left and Arfur tells him about two weeks ago. Tears welled up in Jimmy's eyes as he cradled his head in his hands.

"What do we do now Jimmy? Go home empty handed?"

"Like fuck we do! Where is Mama?" Jimmy asks angrily.

Arfur makes a gesture with his hands to indicate Mama is sleeping. I was gesturing like mad trying to communicate that we wanted to buy some *smack* and would he mind awfully waking her up. I wasn't impressed with Jimmy's so called Thai language ability. He was speaking in some sort of eastern European accent.

"We a like to a buying some *smack*. Can you wake a uppa your Mama?"

"Jimmy I thought you said you could speak Thai. The only word you're saying is Mama and that's not fucking Thai!"

Arfur kept shaking his head and making the sleeping gesture. There we were, the two stooges in the middle of the worst slum in Bangkok, with Jimmy as the interpreter, and all Arfur could say was Mama was asleep.

"Well fucking wake her up!"

Jimmy told me to calm down but I was getting edgy. This deal was supposed to be cut and dried. Instead, I was stuck in this shit-hole with some toothless old clown, his sleeping Mama, and the *Mongol hordes* waiting outside. Arfur pointed to a little *Buddhist* shrine in the corner with a picture of Mama.

"Mama's fucking dead, arsehole! You hopeless bastard! You couldn't score a root in a brothel! Now what! Now fucking what? You expect this baldy toothless old bastard to score a kilo of *smack*? He can't even speak, the dopey fucker."

I leant over and lifted my shirt so that Arfur could see the money.

"See this Arfur! See this! We want *smack*! Lots of it! Can you do it Arfur?" I drew one kilo in the dust on the ground.

"Can you get us a kilo Arfur? We'll pay you."

Jimmy was trying to get me to take it easy. I wasn't having it.

"Fuck! We've got flights to catch tomorrow night. I am sick of you and all your fuck-ups! How long have you known Arfur, Jimmy?"

"About a year."

"Do you trust him?"

"I suppose so"

"So let's get this fucking over with." Arfur goes off and we wait in the shack.

"You didn't have to show him the money."

"It was the only way he would get off his lazy arse. How come you call him Arfur anyway? That's not his real name is it?"

"Of course it's not his real name! I named him after his disease."

"Oh yeah? What disease is that?"

"Arfuritis!"

Arfur came back fifteen minutes later with a different guy. The guy told us he could get us a kilo. We agreed on a price and he told us to follow him. He took us off deeper into the slum and of course more and more people were following us by now. We went inside another shack where there was about ten men sitting down. Most of them were *chasing the dragon*. We sat and talked some more while the other guy went off to get the stuff. He came back ten minutes later, but instead of being in one packet, the *smack* is in gram-sized plastic bottles. How were we going to transport a thousand plastic bottles out of the slum? We checked out the *gear* and it was really good. Jimmy told me to hand over the money.

"You must be fucking mad Jimmy! Hand over the money? No fucking way. Look mate, the stuff is good but how about we get the fuck out of the slum before we hand over any money?"

The Thais debated over this for a while then finally agreed to our terms. One of them got up and told us we were to follow him whatever happened. We got outside the shack and started moving as quickly as we could through the dark slum. Things got a bit panicky. Somebody shouted police and our man took off at a sprint. I told Jimmy to jump on my back and started running after our man with him hanging on for dear life. We were running through the shadows and over rickety bridges with voices calling at us from the shadows. There were two guys on motorbikes waiting, revving up the bikes. Everyone was in a panic, screaming at us to get on the bikes and go. We jumped on them and got the hell out of the slum. Jimmy was on the bike in front of me, holding onto the driver with one hand, and onto his crutches with the other, as these guys drove us speedily through the chaotic traffic of night-time Bangkok. They took us to some scummy little apartment to do the changeover.

I still wasn't happy. I wanted the stuff transported back uptown so we could do the changeover there. The Thais said there were too many coppers in our area and wouldn't do it. I came up with an idea. There were two girls in the room and I reckoned even Jimmy could hold his own with them, so I made a suggestion. We call a taxi, then the two girls get in the car with Jimmy and the *smack*. I would then hand over the money and jump in the front seat of the car. The girls would come uptown with us and we would give them some money for the delivery.

It seemed to be the only solution. I wasn't handing over the money and the guys wouldn't come uptown with us. It wouldn't look so conspicuous with girls. The girls put on big army-style jackets with lots of pockets, and we made sure they put all the bottles in. The plan worked. We got into the cab and took off towards Banglapooh. The girls thought it was all a big joke and kept giggling in the back of the car. Jimmy seemed very agitated and told the girls to shut up.

"Jimmy, relax man. They're only young girls. They'll be OK."

"I think they are planning to run away with the stuff! They keep laughing."

"Jimmy, chill out for fuck's sake! They're probably laughing at the size of your dick. I'll knock them both out if they try anything."

"We can't bring these girls back to a backpackers' hostel. Too many people will look at us!"

"What about that whore the other day? It was OK to get her into the guesthouse?"

"Yes. But she wasn't carrying a kilo of *smack!*"

"Yes! But at least these two aren't dressed up like Christmas tree fairies. We could slip up to the room with them, no problem."

"I don't want them to know where we stay. I don't trust them!"

"Yeah, whatever Jim. You're the boss."

We got to Kaosan road and the girls were really giggly. We got out of the cab but the more Jimmy tells the girls to shut up, the more they laugh. We got to the front of the police station at the end of the road, and Jimmy, in his infinite wisdom, decides this is the time to retrieve the *smack* from the girls. He starts grabbing at their jackets.

"Give me the *smack!* Give me the *smack!*"

Of course the girls are shocked. Jimmy wants them to handover the gear out here on the street!

"Go your room," one of the girls says.

"C'mon Jimmy, let's do this in the room man. Not here for fuck's sake!" I tried to convince him but he wasn't having it.

"Give me the fucking *smack!*"

He grabbed one of the girls by the shoulders and shook her. The way I saw it, the girls had no intentions of doing a bunk. I couldn't see why Jimmy had to make this so complicated.

"You want *smack?*" The girls were angry now. "You want you fuckin' *smack?*"

The girls started pulling the bottles out of their pockets and chucking them all over the street. Me and Jimmy were scrambling all over the place trying to pick up the bottles. The police station was less than a hundred meters away and the street was full of backpackers giving us funny looks. The girls were pissing themselves laughing, enjoying the spectacle. I spotted a couple of cops coming out of the station. We managed to get most of the bottles, ending up losing a few, but we had to get out of there pretty sharpish. We got back to Jimmy's room and threw the *gear* onto the bed.

"Jimmy, I am really sorry about your wife and kid, but there was no need to act like such a cunt with those girls. If I didn't know you better, I'd think you wanted to get busted."

Jimmy was acting really morose and it was hard to get a word out of him. We counted the bottles. There were only two or three short. Jimmy set to work immediately. It was hot that night but we had to switch the fan off lest we blow away the magic white powder. We emptied all the bottles into one big pile on a spread out newspaper on the bed. We had to be careful not to drip sweat onto the powder. Stripped down to our jocks because of the intense heat, we worked through most of the night doing the packing. My job was to take a small bowl and put about five or six grams in the bowl, then add a tiny bit of rubbing alcohol, which made the *smack* slightly moist and turned it brown. It makes the *smack* pliable and shrinks it into smaller lumps instead of massive amounts of dry powder. Of course, I had my reservations about the gig.

"What if I need a shit on the plane, Jimmy?"

"You won't. The *smack* is the best shit stopper around. When we get to Japan we stay off the gear for one night. Take plenty of laxatives. And if all else fails drink a bottle of cooking oil."

"And what happens if none of those things work? What happens if something bursts?"

"Then you're fucking brown bread mate."

169

I have to admit Jimmy did take charge here and carried out most of the work. He seemed to know what he was doing and it could be said he did the work of three men. The fucking *Marx Brothers*.

36

D.E.A.

JIMMY AND I managed to get a couple of hours kip. When we eventually woke up, we immediately started swallowing the big pile of plastic pellets that lay in front of us. The first couple of pellets were hard to get down, but after that it wasn't too bad. I suppose it took a couple of hours before we had ingested all the gear. Now it was time to get ready for the run. We had booked our flights separately. For obvious reasons, it was not a good idea for us to be sitting next to each other on the plane. It was now time to get into character and chose the appropriate costumes.

Jimmy didn't have to worry too much about how he looked because people in general were very helpful towards him due to his physical disabilities. At airports in particular, officials would help him carry his bags. He tried a Hawaiian shirt first. It looked great with his tan but it was just a bit too loud. He didn't want to draw any undue attention, so between us we chose him a dark blue *Fred Perry* shirt and a neat pair of jeans.

Myself, on the other hand, had a more difficult task masking my dodgy demeanour. At first I considered wearing a business suit, but we had heard rumours that there were American *Drug Enforcement Agency* officers working out of Bangkok Airport. An Asian copper might not be able to tell that I wasn't kosher, but any Western copper worth his salt would take one look at me and suss that I wasn't an international businessman. After considering the skint traveller look, this was also thought to be a bit iffy for Japan. If a person landed in Japan dressed like a toe-rag, they tend to ask to see your money and want to know how long you plan to stay. Shit like that, I could do without; I couldn't afford any hassle. My intention was to glide through immigration, hoping that I had the bottle to get past customs, and that I wouldn't give myself away with telltale beads of perspiration or by shitting myself!

The flight we were to be on was the cheapest Bangkok to Tokyo flight we were able to get – *Egypt Air*. We presumed the flight would be full of stinky, hippy, dreadlocked travellers, coming to flog sea shells or whatever on the streets of Tokyo. It was therefore prudent to try and dress accordingly, so I opted for a pair of white jeans, a denim shirt and loafers. Tasteful but not flash and definitely not business like.

"What do you reckon?"

"Luvverley. But you might wanna get yourself a bit of tomfoolery." Jimmy gave me his golden *Buddha* on a chain to wear round my neck.

"You can't be giving me that man! It must be worth a fortune."

"Either you have it or it goes in the bin mate. That bitch gave it me and I don't want fuck all else to do wiv 'er!"

The time came to depart for the airport. From this moment on, and throughout the entire flight, we would completely ignore each other, until we met at our small room in Tokyo. As we walked out into Kaosan Road with our bags, we wished each other luck as we went our separate ways, giving each other a final nod before getting into our respective taxis. Arriving at the airport, I located the check-in for *Egypt Air*, where there was a long line of people already queuing, mostly threadbare, broke-looking, smelly, hippy travellers. A few people in front of me was Jimmy; his cab must have sailed through the traffic, unlike mine. The check-in process was unbearably slow, as many of the hippies seemed to be checking in sackfuls of trinkets and seashell necklaces.

From the corner of my left eye I could see there were two white guys with short-cropped hair and wearing dark suits walking towards the line. Obviously *old bill!* You could smell the bastards as they walked slowly and deliberately with their hands behind their backs. One of them starts from the front of the line and the other from the back, asking each passenger questions as they walk past.

"Where are you going, Sir?" Suit is talking to me.

"Do I know you?"

"Don't get smart." He pulled out his badge. It said D.E.A.

"Excuse my ignorance sir. But what exactly does D.E.A. stand for?"

"*Drug Enforcement Agency.*"

"Oh, I'm terribly sorry sir. I didn't realise. You're a policeman. Drugs? Oh yes, of course. Bangkok, right? Lot of drugs here. Now I understand. I think you guys do a wonderful job man. If you ask me they can hang the filthy *junkie* bastards."

"What are you going to do in Japan?"

"I work as a fashion designer in London. My company is opening a new shop in Tokyo and they want me to be there for the opening. Should be fun!"

"Have you ever been to Tokyo?"

"Yes sir! Many times. And a mighty fine place it is sir."

He gave me a dirty look and walked on down the line. Curly-tailed bastard should be out catching criminals. The cops met about halfway down the line. They never even looked at Jimmy, but both looked at me again for a bit, so I smiled and nodded at them and gave them the thumbs up.

37

GAME OVER

AFTER CHECKING IN I sat in the departure lounge dreading every second, expecting that any moment someone would come up to me and tap me on the shoulder.

'What if something bursts inside me? What if they're waiting for us at Tokyo Airport?'

A packet of *smack* was readily available for my journey, as I knew I just wouldn't have been able to face the ordeal without it. With the *smack* burning a hole in my pocket I went off to the toilets for a swift *sniff*. Jimmy was close on my heels; he was knocking on my cubicle door.

"C'mon, mate! Please! Give us a sniff man! Please!"

I opened the door and let him inside the cubicle with me.

"For fuck's sake man, we are supposed to be ignoring each other not sharing the same fucking toilets." However, I gave him a small line.

"Can I have a bit more man? I'm fucking scared!"

"Jimmy, take it fucking easy, OK. Just stay calm and we'll be all right."

"Let me have a bit more man... For the journey..."

"No Jimmy, fuck you! That's enough. I am not carrying you off the plane. Now fucking chill out."

A voice announced the departure of our flight. I left the toilet in a hurry, trying to put a bit of space between me and Jimmy.

When we boarded the plane, Jimmy was in the row opposite me. After take-off they served the meal and I picked at it, pretending to eat it, but I saw that Jimmy was not having the same problem. He was wolfing it down. Turning around, he looked at me as he shoved the sticky dessert down his throat. The look in his eyes was one I had never seen on his face before. What the fuck was he playing at? He was the one who told me it could be lethal to ingest food after swallowing the *gear*, yet here he was cramming it down his own throat.

Deciding to go to the toilet, I closed the door behind me and put some *smack* on the foil for a *chase*. I didn't want to *sniff* it because I had to take it easy now and wanted to lower the dosage. It wasn't a good idea to be completely out of it when we landed in Tokyo. It was possible to smoke in the toilet of the plane by pulling the plug out of the sink and blowing the smoke into the sinkhole as it sucks in the air. As usual, I had brought too much, and sadly this would mean I would probably have to flush some of it down the toilet before we landed. Just as I was about to vacate the cubicle there was a knock at the door and I heard Jimmy's urgent whispering.

"Open up man! Keep me some." I thought Jimmy was being a complete arsehole. I quickly put the stuff away and came out of the toilet.

"Jimmy what the fuck is wrong with you. I gave you some."

"I'm scared man, Gimme a bit more!"

I handed him the packet and waited outside the toilet. Fucking greedy prick had finished his own *stash* and now he was into mine. I hated all this; bringing attention to ourselves, but what could I do? Jimmy was being a complete pillock. There was no other choice but to humour him.

A few seconds later he emerged from the toilet with a big stupid vacant grin on his face. I put my hand out, expecting the return of what was left of the *smack*, only to be given a bemused smile and his comment.

"I finished it."

What a clown. That was it! I was having fuck all more to do with him. From now on he was on his own. Jimmy got back to his seat and fell asleep, slobbering all over himself. Eventually the plane started its descent into Tokyo and I went over and nudged him awake. His eyes were rolling around in his head and he was dribbling out of his mouth. Completely banjoed!

The plane landed and I got off as quickly as I could, avoiding any contact with Jimmy, who was having great difficulty standing up. There was no problem getting through immigration and I waited patiently down at the luggage conveyer for my bag. Although my luggage arrived, I let it run round a couple of times just to see if Jimmy made it. Eventually he came down from immigration, wobbling like fuck. He was all over the place; it was pretty evident that he could hardly even see. Retrieving his bag off the belt, I put it on a trolley and passed it to him to steer, and hopefully in so doing give his body some support.

"Jimmy! Go on man. Walk through customs. I'll meet you on the other side. C'mon man you're nearly there."

I waited, holding my breath, until he eventually managed to push the trolley up to the customs desk, I make my way to the next desk across from him. The customs official asked Jimmy for his passport, however Jimmy was having great difficulty forming any words. With me, there was no problem. I got through easily and proceeded on my way, walking in front of the aisle where Jimmy was still ensconced with the customs officer. Catching his eye, I could see him mouth my name, but no sound was coming out. That's when he keeled over, vomiting blood, puke and pellets of *smack* in front of everyone. He went into violent convulsions on the floor until eventually he stopped moving. Frozen to the spot, my mouth agape at what had occurred, I stared at Jimmy's lifeless body. The customs man looked at me questioningly.

"Your friend?"

I put out my arms like an airplane's wings.

"No sir. No friend of mine. I just met him on the plane."

38

THE WAY OF THE WARRIOR

AFTER THE EPISODE at the airport, things went rapidly downhill. My addiction got totally out of control. Some of the smack I had smuggled in was sold in Tokyo, but I think I had probably stuck most of it up my nose. After swapping a hundred grams of smack for a hundred grams of coke with some dodgy Mexican bloke, I got into freebasing and started smoking about five grams of coke a day, plus sniffing anything between three and six grams of heroin on top of that. If those drugs were converted into cash, I was going through at least two thousand dollars a day. Of course it was a seven day a week habit, because an addict can't afford the luxury of a day off at the weekend. After unloading all my gear in Tokyo I flew back to Thailand. By now I was a complete physical wreck, with less money than I should have had, plus a monstrous habit to feed.

The first week in Bangkok was spent lying in bed all day, getting *stoned* out of my nut and staring at the ceiling. The only time I got up was to go and score some more drugs from the pool hall across the street. My tolerance was such that when I chopped out a line of *smack* to sniff, I had to do circular ones like mosquito coils because the table wasn't long enough. The situation had gotten so bad that I had to go somewhere. Anywhere!

I bought a couple of big bottles of *methadone* and flew down to southern Thailand. I decided to stay away from the tourist areas; I needed space to think and didn't want to get caught up in the party scene. I befriended some fishermen, and one of them said that I could stay in a hut at the back of his house. We sailed together on his little fishing boat which took us out to this little island about an hour from the coast. The first month was a bit of a blur really. I slowly weaned myself off the *methadone*, but was so weak that I slept most of the time, totally drained mentally and physically. The fisherman's wife prepared food for me but my appetite wasn't that great, so I used to give most of my food to this little dog that came into my hut. He was a skinny little tyke with a limp. The fisherman had three other healthy dogs who he fed regularly, but *Skinny* wasn't tough enough so he always went hungry. Taking pity on him, I adopted him and he slept on the floor at the foot of my mattress. Often he would try and get on the mattress with me, but he was covered with fleas so I had to let him know that the mattress was out of bounds with the old rolled up newspaper technique. Neither the fisherman nor his wife could speak English, which I was actually pretty glad of. I was in no fit mental state for polite conversation.

There was no running water so we had to pull buckets from a well beside the fisherman's hut. It didn't take that long before I started feeling stronger, physically at least. But mentally I was still a mess, being anxious, depressed, scared, bored, and lonely. If I hadn't had my saviour in the form of that skinny little dog to talk to, I would have probably topped myself. There was this huge gaping hole inside of me and I didn't know what to do about it. The thought of going back to the real world terrified me. The solitude of this island gave me the chance to have a long hard look at myself. As my strength slowly started to grow, *Skinny* and I would go for short walks. The fisherman warned me that there were huge constrictor snakes in the forest, so for obvious reasons we gave that a miss. There were lots of little quiet beaches and secluded bays along the coastline where I would strip off, swim in the clear blue sea and watch the beautiful tropical fish swimming around me. Here I was, in the *Garden of Eden,* with this huge depressing cloud over my head. *Skinny* used to come and swim too. He didn't limp when he swam so he looked just like a normal dog. He was a great listener was *Skinny;* all my problems were unloaded upon him. I often found myself apologising for laying all this heavy shit on him. I mean, it wasn't his fault that I had failed miserably as a human being. But I had to lay all this crap on someone, and *Skinny* just happened to be there. When I told him war stories of gang fights and violence, his eyes would widen and he looked scared. He didn't really like the violence. Neither did I really, but what else could I have done in those circumstances? It's not as if I could have turned the other cheek. Somebody would have opened it with a *Stanley* blade.

Every morning before sunrise, four *Buddhist* monks in ochre coloured robes would walk through our village in single file carrying their alms bowls. The villagers would put some food in each of their bowls. The little procession looked almost ghostly as they walked through the dark mist in silence, heads bowed, stopping outside the villagers' huts and waiting in respectful silence. The villagers would then stand in a reverent '*wai*' position, hands clasped in front of their faces as if in prayer, while the monks would chant a blessing for them. One time, the fisherman gave me a bunch of bananas and gestured for me to put them in the monk's alms bowl. I did so and also received the blessing from the monk. This became a daily routine and I actually began to look forward to this little ritual. The monks were so calm and serene with real smiles on their faces. There was something about their energies, their auras; they seemed to shine from within, happy and content in their own skins.

One morning I was surprised to see a foreign monk, a black man, among the procession. He was a tall man, maybe late forties, and very, very wide. In fact he was about as wide as a 7ft by 3ft door. This imposing figure stopped outside my hut. I had some rice and fish that the fisherman's wife had prepared for me the night before, so I walked over and placed it in his bowl. I thought the monks were vegetarian but she had convinced me through much gesticulating that it was quite alright to give the monks some fish. The black monk didn't look like the kind of bloke that would suffer fools gladly; he had one of those deeply lined faces with sad brown eyes that had definitely seen some heavy shit. I almost expected him to break into a soul-wrenching version of *'Nobody knows the troubles I've seen'* on the spot.

"I thought that all monks were vegetarian?"

"We is, but we likes our veggies with fish, veggies with rice and veggies with chicken."

He was obviously a *Yank* so I affected my best *Deliverance* redneck accent.

"You ain't from round these parts are ya boy?"

"Who you calling boy? S'pose ya'll gonna start telling black jokes now."

"Don't know any"'

"Course you do smartass, everybody knows black jokes. Now get it off your chest, go on get over with, tell me a black joke, now!"

His manner was suddenly serious and he leaned forward till his face was only inches from mine. His eyes were like black, spinning pools, and they seemed to be sucking me into their darkness. It felt as if I was being hypnotized.

"Tell me a black joke white boy, and ya'll better make me laugh".

I took a step backwards, gasped for breath and held my hands up in front of me. This freak was scaring the shit out of me.

" Ok, ok, I'll tell you a black joke."

"Go ahead'n make my day."

"What's the name of the new *Christian Dior* perfume for black women?"

"Go on, tell me"

"It's called *Eau De Du Da Day*".

The monk let out a huge belly laugh and all the tension seemed to evaporate right there.

"You thought I was gonna whip your ass there son now, didn't you?"

"If I didn't make you laugh maybe you would have"

"Well, maybe I would"

The other monks had finished their alms round now, and had gathered smiling near the path that led back into the woods.

"Are you a *junkie?*"

"Is it that easy to tell?"

"Takes one to know one son, bin there myself. Ya'll want some help with that?"

Something very strange happened to me when he asked that question. I suddenly felt horribly alone and exposed, totally cold and hungry and completely bereft of all direction or hope. A shiver of fear chilled my spine and my voice wavered as I nodded my assent.

"Yeah, I definitely need all the help I can get."

"Ok, I'll ask the Abbot at our monastery if you can come and stay with us. The food's terrible, you sleep on the ground with a wooden pillow, the hours are long and hard, and there is no pay. How's that for an attractive offer?"

"Sounds wonderful, when can I start?

"Ill be back in a couple of days on another alms round. Shouldn't be a problem with the Abbot, we always need someone to do the domestic chores so we can get on with the business of being holy. And off he went into the forest behind the other monks.

Two days later the monks' ghostly silhouettes appeared from the mist of the forest. The black monk came over and asked me if I was ready, then handed me some plastic bags full of food to carry. We waited for the other monks to finish their alms rounds then we followed them on a small path leading into the forest.

"How long have you been a monk and how should I formally address you and the other monks?" I asked.

"The answer to the first question is fourteen years. You can address everyone as *Phra* except the Abbot; you call him *Ajan* which means teacher."

"Is *Phra* the Thai word for monk?"

"That's correct"

"Don't you have individual names?"

"We do but they are very long and complicated *Pali* names which you will find very difficult"

"What's *Pali?*"

"*Pali* was the language spoken by the *Buddha* 2,500 years ago in India. All his teachings have been preserved in *Pali* and all monks have *Pali* names. It's a tradition."

"So what's your *Pali* name then?"

" *Phra Buddadassa.*"

"Which means?"

"Slave of the *Buddha.*"

"Oh that's rich; first you want to knock me out for joking like a redneck, and yet you chose a name that most of your generation was running away from. Elijah Muhammad, Cassius Clay, Malcom X, and Louis Farrakhan."

"Monks don't choose their names; they are bestowed upon them at ordination."

"Can't you protest?"

"I have seen many foreign monks ordained in Thailand, then begin to fight against the very system they volunteered to become part of. Of course there are many things I disagree with within the whole hierarchal, patriarchal, xenophobic, misogynic makeup of *Buddhism* in general, not only in Thailand but all over Asia. I was in the *Marine Corps* in Vietnam. I stayed in Thailand after the war, and spent years hanging off a needle trying to blot it all out. We committed heinous crimes under orders on a daily basis; we were worse than animals. Then they give you your discharge papers and send you on your way. I spent years being angry at the 'system' for sending me there. I became a forest monk because I love the solitude. Only in the silence can I face my personal demons. If I was a monk in the city I would have to attend an endless round of weddings, funerals and birthdays, where the monks are wheeled in to chant blessings then whisked off to the next function. I didn't join up to become some cartoon giver of blessings. At least as a forest monk I am afforded the opportunity to spend many long months in silence and contemplation"

"Is that your only contact with the outside world, the alms round in the village?"

"That's more than enough contact for me. Even that is enough to stir up feelings of anger and resentment."

"Why?'

"Look at all that extra food you have in those plastic bags. A monk is only supposed to accept enough food to fill his alms bowl, but the dirt poor villagers insist on giving us far more than we can possibly eat. You see, Thais believe that monks are possessed with supernatural powers and can ward off evil spirits and bring good luck. Lay people in Thailand consult the monks on everything from domestic disputes to asking them what lottery numbers will come up. They believe they are earning merit by being generous to the monks, and that they will reap the benefits in the afterlife. It makes me sick to see these poor families with under-nourished children give their choicest pieces of meat and fish to the monks, while they subsist on a handful of rice and bananas."

"Why do they believe monks have supernatural powers?"

"It wasn't too long ago that monks were just wandering nomads who camped out in the jungles and mountains and faced the wilderness alone. Thailand only really became centralized in the fifties. Up until then there was no common language or means of mass communication, no state sponsored education. Monks were schooled in many disciplines including medicine, astrology, music and swordsmanship, and it was the monks who taught in the village schools and provided education free of charge. Sons of the nobility learned discipline from the monks. Most places weren't accessible by road, and people travelled by boat along the rivers that criss-cross through the dense jungle. Monks would cover great distances and encounter many hazards, including wild animals, bandits, and tropical illnesses. Their ecological knowledge made them experts on medicinal plants and the curing of illnesses. The villagers would seek them out for their knowledge and advice"

"What about the snakes and the bandits, did the monks do martial arts?"

"A long time ago, yes, but the tradition kind of died out when firearms were invented. You're probably thinking about the Chinese monks in the *Shaolin Temple.* That's a different tradition, although the *Buddhist* teachings came from the same source, India."

"*Kung Fu* came from India?"

"A Sri Lankan monk named Bhoddidharma travelled to China to spread the teachings of the *Buddha.* He saw that the temples were being raided constantly by bandits and that the monks couldn't defend themselves.

185

Bhoddidarma began to teach them martial arts. He is renowned as a great sage who very rarely spoke, and when he did it was with short sharp answers that cut to the quick."

"Is that because he was Indian and couldn't speak Chinese?"

"I had never thought of that."

"What about the Thai monks? How did they deal with bandits and wild animals."

"They practice developing energy they call *metta*, or love and kindness. They eventually become adept at radiating this energy towards other beings. When I was in a monastery in north-east Thailand there was an elephant that was damaging the crops and trampling the huts of a nearby village. The villagers came and asked the Abbot for advice. The next day the Abbot went down to the village and sat in silent meditation, transmitting *metta* energy all around. Sure enough the elephant came rampaging into the village and came charging straight towards the Abbot. Just at the last moment the elephant halted in front of the Abbot, then walked meekly away. It never came back after that to bother the villagers."

"Did you actually see it happen?"

"Unfortunately no, it was my turn to sweep the leaves from the paths that day."

"I wouldn't have missed that for the world. What a great spectator sport. Imagine it, 'roll up, roll up, and watch the monk get gored by the charging elephant.' You could have taken bets."

We eventually arrived at a clearing in the forest and I took in the surroundings of my new home. The monks lived in little makeshift huts or *kuti's*, which were dotted around the main meditation hall. This was a bamboo structure with a thatched roof and no walls. My *kuti* consisted of an open umbrella covered with a mosquito net which was draped over a straw mat on the floor, complete with a nifty little lump of wood for a pillow. I thought *Buddhism* was about relieving suffering, but this looked dangerously like a bit of good old *Christian* hair-shirting to me. A crown of thorns and a couple of spear marks in the kidneys and I'd be on my way. 'He truly was the son of God.'

Buddha's slave, or *Spartacus* as I had renamed him (not to his face), introduced me to all the other monks one by one. There were probably about twenty five in all. Monks don't do the handshake thing so I politely *wai'd* each one in turn. We then entered the Abbot's *kuti* and he introduced himself as *Ajan Dharmavidoupacarasaranamsadusadu*... or something like that. He was a lovely little man with smiling eyes and a very calm, serene air about him. He spoke in very deliberate halting English.

"Welcome to our forest retreat. *Phra Buddassa* has told me about you. We are preparing for a three-month silent retreat which the monks do every year during rainy season in the tradition of the *Buddha*. The meditation will end when the white lotus is in bloom. Sitting meditation will probably be quite difficult for you in the beginning, so *Phra Buddassa* will instruct you in walking meditation"

"How will meditation help me come to terms with addiction?"

"Addiction is clinging, mental and physical. It is clinging that makes us suffer. Most people spend their lives running around in circles, clinging to false ideas and opinions. This fortifies their sense of alienation. Meditation is letting go, it is transcending or suspending the thinking mind. You must practice repeating the words, '*Not me, not mine.*' Everything is in constant flux, all things are impermanent, the past is history, and tomorrow never comes. There is only here and there is only now. Have you ever seen a farmer catch a monkey?"

"No I haven't. We don't really have monkeys in Scotland, although there are quite a number of Burberry apes."

"The farmer will make a tiny hole in a coconut then push some squashed bananas through the hole. He then ties the coconut to a tree and waits for a monkey to come along. When the monkey pushes his hand through the hole to grab the fruit, his clenched fist is too large to release himself from the hole. The monkey is so focused on taking the fruit, that he doesn't realize that if he only opened his fist he could escape. The farmer can then capture the monkey. Our thoughts are similar to the monkey clinging to the fruit. Our minds can be poisoned by false concepts which make us suffer. Let go of clinging, '*Not me, not mine.*'"

I thanked the Abbot for his pearls of wisdom and headed back to my *kuti*. But I still couldn't quite work out the connection between my smack habit and a monkey with his hand stuck in a coconut. *Spartacus* was sweeping some leaves from the path so I put the question to him.

"The Abbot just tried explaining the concept of 'letting go' to me, but to be honest it seems a bit impractical in real life. '*Not me, not mine.*' What about my wallet, or my girlfriend? Do I just let people take whatever I have?"

"No, that ain't letting go, that's running away. There's a huge difference. A coward dies a thousand deaths, a hero dies but one. Running away is the coward's *modus operandum*. 'I don't like this wife and kids so I'll leave her and get some new ones.' That's crap. What we're talking about here is serenity or equanimity. Developing the ability to internalize your power, and not have it stolen by every little problem that comes into your orbit. Be detached but not indifferent. Don't dwell on the past, 'cause it's already happened. True forgiveness means giving up all hope of a better past. And don't worry about the future, cause it might not happen. And if it does happen, then it probably won't be how you expected it anyhow."

Spartacus outlined my duties for the next couple of weeks before the three-month meditation session was to begin. I would accompany the monks on their alms round every morning and help carry the food offerings back to the retreat. At least I would get to see *Skinny* every day, but the thought of trudging through the dense jungle in the dark wasn't very appealing. My strategy would be to stick as close as possible to the venerable monks and keep my eyes peeled for large reptiles. If perchance a large constrictor should be on the hunt for some *petite dejuener,* he would be fed a live monk or two, while I had it on my toes. At least on the way back I would have some bags full of food to throw at them.

When we got back from the alms round, me and some other Thai volunteers would help divvy up the booty, and present the monks with their only real meal of the day. Sometimes they would have a bit of fruit for lunch but they are forbidden to eat after midday. They can only accept food which is offered to them, and it is polite to offer the food with two hands. Eating at the same table as the monks became quite complicated, because monks cannot help themselves to a dish that a lay person has touched until it is re-offered to them again with two hands. Luckily they didn't use condiments or it could have really gotten out of hand.

'Could you re-pass the salt again, *Phra Spartacus.*'

'Only if you offer it to me first'.

There were morning and evening chanting sessions which I found hard to follow. I was given a booklet, but after the *Pali* chant it would then be chanted in the Thai language, which for some odd reason took twice as long as the *Pali* chants. It might has well have been double

189

Dutch for all the sense it made to me. I did however begin to recognize a few of the repetitive sounds. When I asked *Spartacus* why they kept repeating the same stuff over and over, he sarcastically quipped that perhaps the *Buddha* had been a bit deaf. He could be a pernicious bugger when he felt like it right enough, thon *Spartacus* bloke. Still, he was a bit more down to earth than all this metaphysical *'Not me, not mine'* claptrap.

Chanting proved to be excruciatingly boring, and walking through the jungle wasn't exactly a walk in the park, if you'll pardon the expression. The least pleasant duty had to be setting fire to the monk's *number two's* every morning, specially after *Phra Pong* had been in there. I began to make up a few nicknames for the monks according to their little idiosyncrasies. There was *The Terrible Venerable*, who was always pissed of about something or other, and then there was *Phra Thunder Cloud*, who always looked like he was going to explode when he meditated. *Phra Flip-flip* had two left feet, and always got his flip-flops mixed up with everyone else's. The Abbot on the other hand was a lovely bloke, but I called him the *Venerable General*, because whenever he showed up everyone pretended to look busy.

Brother Ladyboy, or *Phra Poof*, was very effemininate and always winking at me. The Thai people are very tolerant of ladyboys; there doesn't seem to be much discrimination in wider society against them. Ladyboys are pretty much accepted in everyday life, and it's not unusual to find these he-shes filling your normal nine-to-five jobs. Apparently, at a certain time of life, Thai fathers take their young boys aside and have a word in their shell-like about approaching adulthood. A typical coming-of-age conversation between a proud Thai father and his two young sons might go something like this.

"You, young lad, have proved to be a noble warrior and a great martial artist, and I am sending you to the best *Muay Thai Kickboxing* academy in all of Thailand, to train in the tradition of the noble king's bodyguards. You, on the other hand, *Jessie Annie*, will be getting your cock cut off, get a new pair of tits, and begin work as a pole dancer. (What came first, the Thai girl or the pole?)

I began to get used to my daily routine of walking for alms, sweeping leaves, burning shit, chanting and trying to meditate. Sitting meditation was difficult, just like the Abbot had said. I tried to practice being mindful and aware while walking, eating, meditating and showering. *Phra Spartacus* had taught me walking meditation. He said he had used it as antidote for the marching he learned as a young *Marine*. Basically it is a very slow method of walking and being constantly aware of the position of the foot. I found it very relaxing and began to spend long periods of time in walking meditation. At least in walking meditation the eyes remain open. Whenever I closed my eyes in sitting meditation, I would be haunted by unpleasant memories of the past and just get agitated. It certainly didn't make me feel relaxed.

I had been forewarned by the Abbot that the coming long meditation would be similar to lancing a tropical boil. After the first step of bursting the boil, I would then begin to squeeze the pus of my memories to the surface. It was going to be a painful process, but if I remained mindful and detached throughout the process and didn't allow myself to be dragged by the emotion and anger, I would emerge much relieved and stronger, having purged myself of these damaging poisons that had long since clouded my mind. He gave me another couple of analogies. One was of a jar full of water with a muddy residue on the bottom. The mud remains on the bottom until the jar is shaken. Meditation would be like shaking the jar and the dirt of my defilements would rise to the surface. Muddy jars and tropical boils didn't sound like a lot of fun, so I asked *Spartacus* for his take on what I was about to let myself into.

"Imagine yourself in a small boat and there's a hurricane approaching. It's too late to escape, so your only choice is to lash yourself to moorings and hunker down till the storm passes. During the storm you will be confronted by all kinds of events that have happened throughout your life."

"What, like Dorothy in the Wizard of Oz?"

"Yup, damn right, a frightened little bitch just like Dorothy, and this sure as hell ain't Kansas."

Spartacus was beginning to get on my tits a bit with his 'been there, done that' attitude. Sure he was a war vet and obviously a closet psychotic nutcase, but I was veteran of a few wars of my own, and I really didn't see why his experiences were any more relevant than mine. Things between us started to deteriorate when he insisted that I sweep leaves at all hours of the day, when all I wanted to do was lie down rest in the shade. The problem with sweeping the paths was that it was a never-ending task. As soon as I had finished, I had to start over again, because the paths would fill up again with falling leaves. He said that it was for my own good, and that in my sensitive mental state inactivity was detrimental.

At least twice a day he would catch me asleep under a tree and bark at me to stand to attention. He ran the sweeping detail like a military operation. My broom was a thin piece of bamboo with a few sparse pieces of twigs lashed to the bottom; totally ineffectual for sweeping. He would creep up on me and would force me to repeat the rifle creed of the United States *Marines*.

> "Shoulder your broom, soldier. Repeat after me!
> This is my broom.
> There are many like it but this one is mine,
> My broom is my best friend, it is my life!

I must master it as I master my life.
My broom without me is useless.
Without my broom I am useless.
I will learn it weaknesses, its strengths,
its parts and its accessories.
I will ever guard it against weather and damage.
I will keep my broom clean and ready,
even as I am clean and ready.
We will become part of each other.
We are the masters of our enemy.
We are the saviours of my life.
So be it, until there is no enemy but peace."

The problem with *Spartacus* was that you couldn't tell if he was being serious or not. Just like when I first met him and he told me to tell him a black joke or get knocked out. One minute he would be laughing and joking, and the next thing he would be giving you the thousand yard stare. He was half a lump and I really didn't fancy standing toe-to-toe with him, but if he kept up this toy soldier routine he would end up wearing my fuckin' broom.

My broom became more and more dilapidated every day as Drill Sergeant *Spartacus* forced me to repeat the words of the broom creed. I really couldn't give a fuck about the leaves anymore and began to hate sweeping with a vengeance. Eventually nearly all the bamboo twigs had fallen of the end of the broom, rendering it completely useless. I was hiding out at the edge of the camp, swiping at the leaves like I was swinging a golf club, and muttering under my breath at what a stupid fuckin' waste of time it all was. I turned round and found the smiling Abbot standing directly behind me.

"How are you enjoying your stay with us?"

He could see by my face that I was fuming with anger and in a great state of agitation.

"It's the leaves *Ajan*. I sweep them and more fall and I have to sweep them again. Look at this broom they gave me. It's useless, how am I supposed to sweep anything with this?"

The Abbot took a second to think, then looked at me with his smiling brown eyes and said, "Suffering." Then he turned and walked off down the path.

It was like being hit by a bolt of lightning. When *Buddhists* talked of suffering I had always thought it was because it was an Asian third-world religion, and suffering meant the physical suffering brought on by poverty and disease. That wasn't what he meant by suffering. He meant mental suffering. I was just like the monkey with my hand stuck in the coconut, clinging to the belief that I was too good for this sweeping lark, and driving myself nuts over it. How many times in my life had I suffered mental anguish over things I couldn't accept? Leaves were to be swept and I was to be the sweeper. End of story. There are two types of problems in the world; ones you can do something about, and ones you cant. So what was I waiting for? *Spartacus* appeared before me as if by magic and started to recite the broom creed.

"Repeat after me. This is my broom."

"Hang on just a second there, Drill Sergeant. I have a confession to make. I haven't been looking after my broom. It is not clean and ready as I am not clean and ready. Would you mind showing me how to fix the end of it so that I can actually sweep with it?"

"Well done soldier. I knew you'd come round in the end. Let's go and find some twigs to lash to the end of that sad excuse for a broom."

Spartacus began to give me instructions in sitting meditation. He told me that you don't just sit there, you have to be focused. There were many types of meditation, but the general idea was to focus on one point. These monks had been told to focus on their breath. That was all the instruction they received. Observe the coming and going of the breath. This technique was called *Anapasati* in the *Pali* language.

He told me to close my eyes for five minutes and focus only on my breath. It was a lot harder than I thought. My mind raced this way and that; it was almost impossible to keep focused on just my breath. He said I should try to develop a keen and constant awareness of the sensations of the breath, and to remember that this was not a breathing exercise but an awareness exercise. That my concentration and awareness had been shot to pieces by drug abuse. There was a huge hole in my aura and he believed that the *heroin* had made my spirit leave my body. I didn't really believe in all this stuff because my only experience of religion or any kind of spiritualism had been battered into me by frustrated old bags who shouldn't have been allowed anywhere near children. We were taught that God was this terrifying Old Testament cartoon character who sent down plagues of locusts on little boys' heads for lusting after the posteriors of cuteness. Here I was from a so called technologically advanced, free-thinking Western democracy, and the thought police had terrified me from day one with this big, beardy father sitting in the clouds keeping his cosmic scoreboard. By *Catholic* standards I was well into minus on the sin front, and I had a snowball's chance in Hell of getting into Heaven.

Spartacus explained to me the beauty of being in the present moment. The *Buddhists* call it mindfulness. We might think of it as awareness. By doing everything in slow motion, the monks were building up and strengthening their awareness, being totally focused and concentrating on every movement they made. They were being obedient to the moment. He went on to explain that our minds are always scattered every which way. We are either stuck in the past or dreaming about the future. Memory or fantasy? We eat food and read the newspaper at the same time. We try to do ten things at once and we end up doing nothing properly. This technique of observing your breath opens your awareness. The ego drops and consciousness widens. The mind becomes focused and aware and concentrated. Power is internalised and wisdom appears. The conceptual linguistic thought is incapable of seizing and expressing the absolute, and that suspension or transcendence of conceptual thinking is realization. He said that we have invested the thinking mind with a reality it doesn't possess, that is, an ultimate reality. He described the scattered mind as a drunken monkey that had been stung by a wasp. The mind is like a monkey, which jumps from branch to branch on a tree, and the idea of meditation is to leash the monkey mind. Once the mind becomes gentle and harmonious by diligent practice, bad memories no longer have the ability to make you sad, depressed or angry, because you are now seeing them with a balanced mind and you let them go. The idea is to develop a choiceless dynamic awareness. With active surrender we come to understand that our inner dialogue blocks the light of our natural wisdom. It is not mind control, because the mind cannot be controlled or suppressed.

The mind is like a freight train thundering past your mind's eye 24 hours a day. In every carriage there is a different thought, a constant parade of the inner working of the mind. Real power comes from not being dragged by the emotion. Just observe and let this train of thoughts go round and round, without identifying or being pulled in any direction by any of them. This technique allows us to let these things go and not be a slave to our emotions. He explained that through practicing this meditation and mindfulness, some monks had developed their physic abilities. Some could detect sickness in people, others could read minds. These powers may have been widely exaggerated, but a lot of people have gone to tremendous lengths to try and discover the powers within themselves. People have made pacts with the devil, drank human blood, slept in graveyards, but *Spartacus* maintained that these gifts can only be given, and there was no magic formula that worked for everyone. It was a famous *Buddhist* story that a monk who had many magical powers was asked how he developed these skills. He answered that it came about by chopping wood and carrying water. By the magic of mindfulness. By being completely aware and in the present moment whatever it is you do, be it washing dishes or carrying bricks. If you can surrender to the moment completely and unconditionall,y then that in itself is magic.

He called emotion the chief hooligan, and the five senses the five thieves. One of the senses can trigger an emotion, and the next thing all-over power is drained. I asked *Spartacus* what to do if someone or something crops up in our mind's eye and makes us angry. He told me I must cut off this image and go back to observing my breath. If I stay with the image I will be dragged by the emotion and my harmonious mind will be shot to pieces. Gradually, day by day, *Spartacus* guided me through the minefield of my emotions, my personal valley of darkness. Bravely venturing where I had previously feared to tread, looking within for answers. I suppose the gist of the teachings was that instead of waiting for divine intervention, I should get on with it myself. It's not as if anyone was trying to convert me. *Buddhists* believe that all religions basically taught the same things. Peace, love and understanding. Most religions believed that God made man, but then they make their own gods and worship their own creations. The problems probably began when politics became mixed up with religion, and governments realised that to control the population's beliefs was to control the population. Truth is a universal phenomenon, not some hidden secret in scriptures or dogma, only to be deciphered by those priestly custodians of incomprehensible truths. Holy people always got up my nose, walking round like they had God's phone number.

It was obvious that I was full of hate, anger, rage and resentment, but I couldn't see my letting these things go, because they were my last line of defense. I wasn't letting any of this go, because when all is lost I still had my anger to protect me. Where I come from we don't use the word surrender. Let your guard down for one second and someone will hit you right on the chin.

I persevered with the meditation and the work but I had some very strong reservations. All this kindness and gentleness was alright in this environment, surrounded by monks, but I couldn't see how this could apply to the dog-eat-dog world that I came from. I know that *Jesus* said that we should turn the other cheek, but look what they did to him. *Jesus's* career only lasted three years, and he was persecuted specifically for preaching love. Maybe it was my conditioning, but I saw all this love and kindness stuff as pretty meek. In an ideal world it would be great to love my neighbours and do unto others, but this is far from being an ideal world, and the idea of repaying anger with kindness or love just didn't wash with me. Unless of course you had some masochistic need to act as society's doormat and let every one trample over and wipe their feet on you.

I was getting used to the silence. I found myself becoming calmer, and I was able to sit longer in meditation without becoming angry, frustrated or bored. The *Venerable General,* or *Ajan Dharmavidoupacarasaranamsadusadu,* would go into a little temple in the woods and meditate completely motionless for three hours every morning. There were some really nasty looking monkeys living in that temple, and anytime I went near them they attacked me. Even when I tried to give them fruit they nearly bit my finger off. The *Venerable General* would just casually stroll into the temple and the monkeys didn't even look at him. He would sit in the *lotus* position and sometimes the monkeys would go and sit in his lap. I asked him how he did this and he said he was generating *metta*, or love and kindness energy toward the monkeys, and that they could feel this. I had actually felt him generate this energy towards me the first time I met him. Otherwise I would have dismissed this as hocus-pocus. It must have been what *Daniel* did in the biblical story when he was fed to the lions. I always suspected the lions just weren't hungry, but then again, if it's so easy to generate anger towards people then surely it was possible to generate love towards someone.

The monkeys wouldn't let me anywhere near the temple even though I attempted to generate this *metta* stuff. The monk told me I would have to peel away a few layers of conditioning before I could uncover this energy, saying that I would first have to let go of my anger.

During the meditation, one starts to become sensitive to sensations in the body. Everything begins to ache and it is very hard to stay still. It can be mind-numbingly boring one minute, then extremely calm and relaxing the next. The idea is to ride the storm and discipline yourself to resist whatever sensations or thoughts come at you. We had a few more days before the three-month retreat was to begin, so I started to meditate some more. A painful sensation between my chest and my left shoulder appeared. I didn't know what it was but I knew it hurt.

I mentioned the pain to the Abbot and he told me that when I start the course the pain would probably increase and magnify. It would also become difficult to control my emotions. Whatever happened, I was to go back to watching my breath and not get dragged back by the chief hooligan, emotion.

By the second day of the three-month silent retreat, the area below my left shoulder hurt so much I had trouble walking and sleeping. I felt wretched, depressed, sad and lonely. I was bored shitless and couldn't see myself getting through this. The midday heat had been so intense. It was just before the rains and the humidity made it almost impossible to concentrate. My mind was racing, being unable to concentrate on my breath. I felt like I was going mad. All these memories and emotions that I forgotten came bounding back to haunt me. Even though I was utterly exhausted, I couldn't sleep a wink, and was totally pissed off at having to spend another whole day meditating or doing things in slow motion. Even the brushing of the teeth had to be done slowly and mindfully. The monk in front of me was normally slow anyway, but now he was completely taking the piss. I forgot I wasn't supposed to speak and told him to hurry up. Of course all the monks turned around and look at me. I had just broken the noble silence rule.

I was in a terrible mood when we sat down to have our bowl of rice for breakfast. I grabbed my plate in defiance and wolfed down the rice, making a loud scraping noise with my spoon, which made all the monks turn and look at me again. I stared them down.

As soon as I sat down to meditate, the pain came back below the shoulder again. It was permitted to seek advice from the Abbot, so I stopped him on the way back to his hut and complained about the pain, telling him how desperately depressed and pissed off I was. He said I should understand that all this negativity I was digging up was actually a good thing because I had something to work with. I should be happy when the anger comes because I can feel what anger does to me. How it makes me hot and twists my organs 'til I boil over with rage. He told me it is easier to defeat a thousand of my enemies than it is to defeat my self. The next time I feel anger I should say, 'Welcome anger,' and just observe and let it go. The anger was like the pus from a tropical boil.

He told me that in Thailand nearly everyone, at some point in their life, becomes a monk for at least a short time. Some unscrupulous people use it as an excuse to hide from the land. Many drugs addicts seek a cure in *Buddhism*, and monks come from all walks of life. He knew about my boxing career, and he asked if I had been a *southpaw*, and what would I do if I wanted to hurt someone. I told him I would line them up with a jab then knock them out with a big left hand. He pointed out to me that many Thai ex-boxers had studied with him, and that it was common for *southpaw* boxers to develop a sickness below the left shoulder. This area is where the punches originated, and where the brain sent a signal to initiate the punch. Along with the signal to punch, the brain also sends anger and aggression.

Years and years of unconsciously sending anger and aggression to this one spot had manifested itself into a sickness in my spirit body, which would later affect my physical body and become a tumour or cancer. He told me that my spirit hadn't forgiven my body for what I had done, telling me to go back and meditate, and that if the pain was so great I should put my hand on the spot and pray.

Sure enough, the pain was excruciating. I put my hand on it to pray. He didn't tell me who to pray to, so I thought I would try them all. I started with a few *Hail Marys* and *Our Fathers*, then I tried a little *Buddhist* chant I had heard. I prayed to *Shiva* and to *Allah*, and apologised to anyone else that I had missed out. It wasn't my intention to incense any deities to divine retribution here. It was just that I had never been much of a praying person, and although I was a *Catholic* by birth, I was in the land of the *Buddha* here.

I was getting really confused about the whole thing. Apparently the *Buddhists* have a very complicated idea of what God actually means, so I didn't know if *Buddha* would be angry if I prayed to God. I figured that if I called Him by all these names, I might get the right one eventually. In this totally confused state I tried to concentrate on my breath, finding sitting in meditation almost impossible. What on earth was I doing here, walking up and down in slow motion with a horrible pain in my shoulder, getting angrier and angrier by the minute? This whole God thing was doing my nut in.

My head was full of images of pain and suffering. Nightmares about this guy dripping with blood hanging off a cross, getting piked in the side with a spear. What the nasty old bags had taught us at primary school - terrifying, dried-up, evil old witches, beating the living crap out of us, taking out their hatred of the whole male race on helpless little boys. All in God's name of course. *Suffer the little children.*

Apparently there are certain *Native American* tribes who don't allow women, or even mothers, to speak or even look directly into the eyes of young braves, for fear of damaging their spirit. That might sound a little extreme, but what about the extremities of intolerance that little male slum-dwellers have to suffer at the hands of middle-aged, middle class, mid-life crisis, menopausal, twisted bitter old hags. Bible in one hand a big leather belt in the other!

My mood wasn't improving. I felt like there was a huge dark cloud above my head. I just wanted to give up and forget the whole thing, wishing I were back at the fisherman's hut. I had been warned that my negativity would be magnified, and not to be dragged down by the emotion. However, the monkey mind was throwing so much bad shit at me, I was drowning in it. At four in the afternoon the Abbot gave a discourse in Thai. After the discourse it was permitted to ask questions, so I raised my hand and asked a question about justifiable anger. I was basically saying that there comes a time in every man's life when he has to stand up and be counted. That action has to be taken. That *Goliath* must be downed.

The monk explained that if you break things down into ultimate matter, anger has a vibration, and that it is destructive whether it is justifiable or not. This made me angrier. I knew that if you put a brick under a powerful microscope in a laboratory, you could probably see that the brick was made up of millions of sub-atomic particles. That was all very well in the laboratory, but if somebody throws that brick at your head, then you had better fucking well duck! Sub-atomic particles or no sub-atomic fucking particles! All this abstract freedom from the bondage of self, '*I'm pink, therefore I'm spam,*' nonsense was really winding me up. What did he know anyway? Farting away in his silent caves, thinking his shit didn't stink. It was alright for them and their loving kindness bollocks on a tropical island. Try that outside the *kebab* shop on Dundee high street at closing time on a Saturday night, or when it's minus twenty degrees and you're lying naked on the cold floor of a jail cell, hardly able to move due to the kicking you had just received from the police.

By ten that night, I was seething with anger. I burst into the Abbot's hut and shouted at him. I told him that my anger was the only thing that got me through life. It was my survival instinct. He tried to explain again that anger hurt me. It was like picking up a burning stick and throwing it at someone. I would have to burn my own hand first. He just didn't get it! I stormed out of his hut and walked off into the jungle, swearing at the top of my voice, kicking and punching trees, throwing branches around. I had every fucking right to be angry! It was my comfort zone. My cushion! I walked for miles and ended up coming out at a little beach. I stayed there the night although I didn't sleep much. I couldn't face the fucking monks with their love and fucking kindness. Showing up at the camp next morning, I looked and felt like a wounded animal, hating all of them. Sanctimonious wankers! I knew I was different. They might think it's cool to let people walk all over them but I didn't. Fuck that for a game of soldiers.

I sat down to meditate and the pain in my shoulder came back immediately. The monkey mind went completely over the top. Jimmy dying, the police, *Borstal*, the violence, my brother's death, my parents, *Jesus*, God, *Buddha* and the stupid monks paying back anger with kindness? No fucking way, not me. Bring it on! Take a fucking shot! Take your best one you bastard, strike me down! Put your fucking hands up and fight like a man! My head was full of images of the coppers laying into me as my brother looked on dying. Didn't he deserve more than to see those fucking animals beat me as he took his final breath? Fucking dirty, lying, no good bastards, all of them. I ran to the edge of the camp and started punching a tree. My hands were bleeding so I started head butting it till the blood ran down my face. I was sweating, screaming, spitting, and crying. Fucking bastard, cunting fucks! All of them! The monks gathered round me but I had a stick in my hand.

"Get the fuck away from me you bastards!"

I put both arms round the tree and started biting the bark with my teeth and growling like an animal. I couldn't stop myself. I was totally fucking mad. The Abbot came running from the temple and told the monks to sit down and chant. I was on my knees now, swearing into the ground, my face covered in mud. Sitting there, I cried my eyes out for what seemed like eternity.

Later that day, I picked up my belongings and thanked the monks, telling them that I just wasn't ready for this. They tried to make me stay because they said it was dangerous to leave in such a tender emotional state, but I just had to get out of there.

39

NICKED

ONCE I ARRIVED back in Bangkok I stayed on Ka-osan road for a couple of weeks. My daily dosage of smack was at least three grams a day and I smoked weed like other people smoked cigarettes. Every day I would wake up in a heap on the floor of my shitty little room, surrounded by empty whiskey bottles, spilled pow-der, crushed out joints, with dried up vomit all down my front. It wasn't a good look. Whatever it was the monks had made me face on the island, I was trying to escape from it now. Running low on funds, I knew the only way out was another drug run to Tokyo. I just didn't fancy scoring in the Klung Toy slum again where I'd gone with Jimmy. One afternoon after waking up in my usual pos-ture, I headed for the pool hall on Kaosan Road to score some gear. My man wasn't around, but there was this other European bloke dangling about, so I asked him if he knew where to score. I had clocked him in the pool hall lots of times. He was obviously a scuzzy junkbag like myself. It takes one to know one. I gave him the dough upfront and waited thirty long minutes in the café oppo-site until he came back with the goods.

We went back to his hotel to use, and of course the old *opiates* began to kick in and we got to talking. He had done a few runs himself, and told me that if I want-ed to score quantity he could get a good price. To cut a long story short the bastard stitched me up. I found out later that he worked hand in hand with the Thai police and the *D.E.A.* His job was to entice people into drug smuggling. Not that I personally needed much entice-ment, but apparently a lot of young travellers down on their luck fall prey to this Swiss snake. He had apparently been busted five years earlier with a kilo of smack and was given a choice; either help the police to entrap oth-er people or face the death penalty.

Since 1974, the Americans had poured 81 million dol-lars into anti-drug assistance in Thailand. These customs officials and cops had to justify their existence. They used criminal gangs or foreign grasses to lure people into working as drug couriers so that it looked as if they were battling the drug problem. Innocent travellers would be cajoled into carrying suitcases from A to B with no idea what was inside. There would be a front-page spread the next day in the newspaper, with smiling customs of-ficials leading some naïve young traveller off to a life be-hind bars. This kept the pressure off the big boys who continued to send containers full of smack all over the globe.

Anyway, the Swiss snake set me up, selling me some *smack* and tipping off the cops. As soon as I checked in at the airport for my flight to Tokyo, two plain-clothes cops grabbed my arms and arrested me. The cops had litmus paper and tested everything I had, including my toothpaste, shampoo and ointment. They found a few *codeines*, which are *opiate* based painkillers, and they asked me if I used *smack*. I just kept denying everything and tried to remain calm. What really got to me were their smiling faces. Every time a new pair of cops came to question me, they would give me this big hungry croc-odile smile, then start the same questions all over again. It was a Sunday night and they were having difficulty locating a doctor to do my X-ray. After about ten hours of this my nose started to run. The shakes and sweats had started to kick in. The pigs knew the symptoms. *Cold turkey* was in the post.

The first signs started off mild, but as the shakes and shivers got worse I felt like I was going to shit myself. That is not a metaphor for fear, I mean this most sincerely folks. After suffering with severe constipation for over a month, the lack of *heroin* over the last few hours was causing a great loosening of the bowels, and I was coming dangerously close to laying a large chocolate log in my pants, the consequences of which would surely have given away the guff. The withdrawals were starting to make me feel really bad; I just wanted to lie down but the pigs kept forcing me to sit up. They were trying to force feed me with something, probably a laxative of some sort, but I kept spitting it out. The cops were slapping and kicking me from every direction. If only they would let me lie down and rest I would feel so much better, but they were having none of it. One guy kept pulling my head back by my hair every time I tried to rest it down on the desk.

"Have you swallowed drugs? You better tell us! You better admit it!"

"No! I didn't swallow anything. Please, let me lie down, just for a minute. Please!"

After about twelve hours, the doctor finally arrived. They picked me up and dragged me off into another room where there was this ancient looking X-ray machine straight out of a *Frankenstein* movie. I was so fucked by this time I couldn't even stand up. My legs had turned to jelly. They held me up for the X-ray, and as soon as they saw the little black balls in my stomach they really laid into me. My face was like a fucking watermelon. I kept trying to curl up on the floor but they would just pick me up again for some more heavy licks.

They asked me if I had anything up my arse. I denied it of course, so picking me up, my lower half was held up for a mug shot. I was struggling as best I could as I didn't want my bollocks exposed to all that radiation, but I was weak as piss so struggling was a waste of time. Must be against the rules though, X-raying bollocks. Not fucking cricket if you ask me. The packages I had stuffed up my arse were spotted. Two hundred grams of pure number four heroin to be precise. They forced me to sit on this elevated toilet thing, tied my hands to the sides, shoved a funnel down my throat and poured in some liquid laxative. It worked like magic. I started shitting, pissing and puking simultaneously.

A few packets of *smack* that hadn't been digested were coming back up out of my mouth; it was a fucking painful process bringing them up again. I sat strapped to that shitter for a good fucking twelve hours. The shit, the blood, and the puke mingled together as the bastards laid into me for being a nasty, evil drug smuggler. They gave me such a beating that I kept drifting in and out of consciousness in a dream-like stupor. I actually wished and hoped that I was dreaming, because every time I came around they gave me another going over.

Eventually, when they thought they could extract no more from my pathetic, naked limp body, I was handcuffed with my hands behind my back and thrown onto the floor of a bare cell. It was a funny sort of heaven just to lie there on the cold floor with my face on the concrete. I was still puking, but the only things that came up were bile, stomach lining and perhaps a lump or two of bone cartilage. I flopped around on the floor like a fish for a few more hours. Some time in the early hours of the morning I began to perk up again. There was nothing in my stomach and I was so hungry I could have eaten the legs off a skinny priest, but I was too scared to move in case the screws clocked me through the peep-hole and set about me again, so I just stayed put. The sun had just begun to creep under the cell door when I heard the footsteps of a guard outside. He rattled his keys for a bit, then opened the door and motioned for me to follow him. I was taken to a shower room where they gave me a bar of horrible smelling chemical soap. I cleaned off all the blood and piss. A T-shirt and shorts were handed to me and I was then cuffed and taken to a police station to be booked. I agreed with everything they said and signed what they wanted me to sign. I was too sick to do otherwise.

After the mandatory seven days in the police station I was moved to *Bombat* prison. The prison guard responsible for checking me in told me to take my clothes off and bend over for an anal probe. He took a rubber glove out of the drawer and I couldn't help but notice that the fingers of the glove were stained brown. There was no way he was going to poke me with that thing, so I told him to either get a clean glove or go fuck himself. That was the first and last time I ever argued with a guard. As a result he called on the help of two other guards, and they proceeded to beat my naked body to a pulp on the cold hard floor. As if this wasn't enough, two of the guards then lifted me by my ankles and spread my legs while the other guard brought his baton crashing down on my groin. I must have passed out at this stage as I woke up naked on a cell floor surrounded by other prisoners. A T-shirt and shorts were lying beside me, and one of the other prisoners motioned for me to put them on. Prison issue uniform, shit brown colour. Two of my teeth were missing and one testicle had swollen up like a tennis ball. What gave those bastards the fucking right?

Every twelve days, we, the prisoners, were cuffed, shackled, loaded into open top cattle trucks and taken for a court appearance. After a sweltering ride through the Bangkok smog, we would arrive at the courthouse where we were herded into sweaty holding pens for the day. I went through this shit five times. It was sheer humiliation being driven through the streets of Bangkok like livestock, having to endure the shouting and jeering from passers by. All day we would have to wait shackled together for fuck all to happen, then be driven back at night to the welcome sight of the big brown glove. When I did eventually get my big chance to appear before the Judge, it wasn't difficult to guess what the outcome would be.

There I stood in front of the Judge, shackled to a gigantic Russian bloke who looked like an extra from Michael Jackson's *Thriller* video. My shit brown uniform smelled like a gorilla's armpit and my hair looked like it had been cut by the council. The trial was conducted in Thai; there was no translator provided. The *Pope* would have looked guilty under those circumstances. I was given two choices. Either plead not guilty and face the death penalty, or plead guilty and get a hundred year sentence, which would be immediately reduced to fifty years. Some fucking choice! Obviously, I chose the latter. My sentence was given and I was sent to the maximum-security jail, Thailand's most notorious monkey house, *Bang Kwan* prison. *The Big Tiger.*

40

THE BARBER

THE WORST PART is waking up in this place. Not that getting to sleep is any picnic either, with the mozzies, flies, lice, bed bugs and the heavy coughing of the TB infested inmates, but at least when you close your eyes it's a few hours respite from hell. The first thing that enters my awareness when I wake up is the sound of a hundred death row inmates dragging their five-kilo leg irons as they are released from their pens by their lazy bastard guards. Some selected inmates, or trustees as they are known, do most of the work for the guards. The guards sleep all day and only wake up for the occasional blowjob or massage with a happy ending from a ladyboy (katoey). We call them the rub-and-tug brigade. They have two toilets in here. One says 'Men', and the other one's for trannys, which says 'Work-in-progress'.

I like to keep myself clean and tidy but even that is difficult in here. There are all kinds of pitfalls to be avoided when going for a scrub. The chutney ferret is an obvious one to avoid. Bum-banditry is rife, and one must guard one's chocolate starfish at all times. Even after death. Apparently the *Bang Kwan* method of ascertaining whether a prisoner is dead or alive, is to ram a long piece of wire up their arse to see if they react. What happened to feeling for a pulse? Beat you to death and shove a coat hanger up your tea towel holder to make

sure they've done a good job. Flagellation and necro-
philia! I've heard of flogging a dead horse but *Bang
Kwan* takes the biscuit.

The shower water we use is pumped from a local
river, and is filthy, poisonous, sewage filled, slimy yuck.
It comes straight into our shower troughs, which are
forty foot long and four feet deep. There are all kinds
of algae, wormlike, bacterial, faeces-eating parasites
in here. The sweltering heat and filthy conditions are a
perfect breeding environment for these living organisms.
They say a hundred prisoners die a month in Thai prisons and that's probably a conservative estimate. The
shower trough is right next to the moat that surrounds the
prison hospital. One day the Thais caught, skinned and
ate a seven-foot python that was living in the moat. The
python had probably been living off the abundance of
frogs, toads and crabs that were living in and around
the shower area. The crabs lived off the dead bits of tis-
sue that the lepers had scraped off their bodies with the
aid of steel rulers. These superfluous parts would fall into
the hospital moat and the crabs would gather under the
lepers' window every day at two in the afternoon, knowing instinctively that this was feeding time. People joke
about lepers playing cards and chucking their hands in,
but here it's true.

There was one story surrounding a certain shower
trough that most foreigners didn't believe. Thais are a
very superstitious bunch, and are always telling stories of
ghosts, spirits and monsters. Hidden dragons in *The Big
Tiger*. Apparently this monster had found its way up from
the river, through the sewage pipes and in to the trough.
Theories abounded as to the genetic make up of the
beast. But the general consensus of opinion was that it
was some sort of mutant crocodile, which was a result of
the gross overfeeding of crocodiles by the Thai army on
the up-river crocodile farms. After the '96 military coup,

hundreds of students and demonstrators went missing, and rumour has it that they were fed to the crocodiles. Escapees from these farms back the story up. A huge gambling industry grew around the monster. Every day at shower time, a new inmate to *Bang Kwan*, still wearing the chains compulsory for the first three months of jail, would be forced to the edge of the trough. Bets would be placed on the victim's chances of getting eaten. The monster usually fed every two or three days, but one time it didn't eat for two and a half weeks. Fortunes were won and lost as the betting increased daily in the hope that the monster would feed. After the authorities closed down the shower trough, we began to wonder if the story was true. Also a few prisoners had been reported missing at role call, yet no one had heard any alarm bells. True or not, who knows? I never actually saw any crouching tigers or hidden dragons, but that's perhaps because they were crouching and hidden. Rather stick needles in my eyes than shower in that trough though.

There are some real desperadoes in here who have to be avoided like the plague. They have been sentenced to one hundred years and will never leave the prison. They have no income, no families, no friends, and no future. They mutilate themselves with knives, and then rub hot ash into the wound to leave a pronounced visible scar. Even the guards steer clear of those bastards. Their savageness and brutality knows no bounds. If a Thai wants revenge on another Thai he hires one of those desperados. If one of these guys gets hold of you it's not going to be a quick, painless death, that's for sure. These cunts get medieval on you. There are people being carted off daily to the morgue, the hospital, and the funny farm, never to be seen again. I was in the hospital ward once. The guy in the next bed to me, a lifer (a hundred years in Thailand), had no arms, no legs, and couldn't speak. People used to call him *Flipper*. I couldn't for the life of me work out what this poor cunt could have possibly done to get life in prison. I found out later that he had been an armed robber, and had been lynched by a crowd who chopped off his arms and legs and doused him with petrol. They had only just set him alight when the police came and put out the flames. He hadn't spoken since. The Judge gave him life. Perhaps in this case, execution would have been kinder.

Being in here reminds me of that movie *Bridge Over the River Kwai*; emaciated prisoners dropping like flies from hunger and disease. Taking away a person's liberty is one thing, but to completely strip them of their dignity for want of a few easily available medicines is over the top. Some of the poor suffering creatures wandering around this prison do not belong in this day and age. Suffering of this magnitude is completely unnecessary. Only the foreign prisoners can afford medicine. The Thais are given a prescription that they can't afford to pay for. Little cuts turn into seeping, pus-filled wounds. The prison authorities don't give a fuck because the prison population is an expendable sub-human work force.

To the outside world, Thailand advertises itself as the land of smiles, paying lip service to their *Buddhist* dogma. But *Buddhism* is supposed to be about compassion. In the West we are brainwashed with the image of cruel, intolerant *Muslims* chopping off women's clits with blunt knives and beheading criminals, but to see people slowly fade in here, to see this freak show of fungal infected growths, of malnutrition, of open seeping wounds, it makes me wonder about this whole compassion business. If I didn't meditate it would all be too much for me. The meditation cushions my psyche against the harshness of reality. That's the only way to survive in here. Stay focused and stay anonymous. Or invisible, if possible!

I was hoping to get into the golden boy amnesty class. You never know your luck. Maybe the government might have a change of heart at some point and include drug traffickers in the amnesties, along with the rest of the baby-eating, mother-killing, paedo-beasts, so I had to stay out of trouble. To show emotion was to show weakness. I had to be inscrutable just like the Asians. I liked that word and looked it up in the dictionary. It comes from the *Latin*, and it means 'wholly mysterious', or, 'that which cannot be penetrated'. That was the image I would try to portray; wholly fucking mysterious.

Know thy enemy. I can't remember who said that but it's an important bit of advice, especially in jail. It wasn't easy trying to get my head around the Thais and the way they operated. The problem with the Thais was, there is no such thing as an honest face. People say they all look the same and it's true. There is a uniformity of expression and physical characteristics amongst them. White people's emotions are written all over their faces, but you never know what a Thai is thinking. It is this unpredictable facet of the Thais that one has to be wary of. You never know when they are going to lose it and are best avoided. The one guard who seemed to be okay was Sonchai. He appeared to actually emulate the teachings of the *Buddha*, rather than the ceremonial, ritualistic prayers that most of the Thais seemed to be into.

Sonchai was a guard on death row, where one hundred prisoners lived in limbo because the King had put a stay on executions. No-one had been executed for the past nine years, so the best these guys could ever hope for was life behind bars strapped in leg irons. The guards could be bribed to let us into the death row exercise yard for a hair cut from the barber who was a prisoner there. His name was Promas Leamsi. It wasn't that he was a great barber or anything; it was just a break from the monotony of life in prison, a ceremony of waiting in line, sitting in a chair and getting pampered just like in the real world. It was little things like this that made the difference between hanging on to what was left of your sanity and losing it completely. Leamsi spoke excellent English, having spent seven years in the States. He was well liked inside the prison, even by the guards. The area where he cut hair was well swept, his brushes and combs lovingly disinfected, and his scissors super sharp.

Leamsi's little corner was a hive of activity. It was directly adjacent to the Execution Yard, or *'The Place to Relieve Suffering'*, as the sign in Thai read. He would cut the guards' hair for free and they would turn a blind eye to the goings on in the corner. Nothing went on in Leamsi's corner without him knowing about it. Like any hustler worth his salt, he made sure he got his end of any business. He wasn't a big tough guy or anything, having that short, stocky build typical of a northern Thai of Chinese decent. He possessed that magical combination of charm, fearlessness and barefaced cheek that allowed him to flaunt the prison regulations.

When I asked him how he fitted this in with his *Buddhist* beliefs, which he held very strongly, he would always give me his interpretation of what the *Buddha* meant by certain things, therefore allowing him to carry on with his shady commercial enterprises with a clear conscience. He could handle himself too. He wasn't one of these little wankers with tattoos and a puffed-up chest who constantly tried to prove their *hardness*. It was just in his manner. He was *hard* and he knew it. So did everybody else. Apart from his dodgy dealings, Leamsi also translated documents for foreign prisoners, liaising between foreigners and guards in general, and helping to arrange appointments with the only doctor available on death row, who was also a prisoner. The Thais called the doctor Hon Chin. We called him *Doctor Death*. As the prison's medical facilities were non-existent, *Doctor Death* was the only alternative. This personification of evil had been found guilty of injecting his wife and two young children with arsenic, killing all three. Infection was rife in jail because of the unsanitary conditions; the smallest cut could turn septic very quickly. If the heat didn't get you, the flies would. Often the choice was between *Doctor Death* and gangrene. On one occasion I had the misfortune of having to visit him concerning a shard of glass in my foot. I was welcomed into his God-forsaken cell/surgery with a half smile, his lips curling to show a row of black gravestone teeth. He squinted through his thick specs at my injured foot. Dirty, long, greasy, sparse strands of hair were plastered to his head. Choosing a blunt, rusty-looking instrument, he started to dig around inside my foot. Wincing with pain I unwisely asked him for some sort of anesthetic. Telling me to hang on, he left the room, returning with two Thais in tow. One of them grabbed me in a headlock while the other one twisted my arms behind my back. *Doctor Death* hissed at me.

"Here's your anesthetic. And if you try to move I will make sure that it really fucking hurts!"

The pain was unbearable as he scrubbed my foot with a wire brush. A month later the wound was still festering, so I wangled my way into the prison hospital where they removed *Doctor Death*'s little souvenir. Two inches of filthy medical gauze that he had stitched inside my foot, which then took months to heal properly!

Most of the conversations in jail centered on release dates, rumours of King's pardons, or exchange programs allowing foreign prisoners to serve their time back in their own countries. But there was no such hope for Leamsi and the other death row inmates. One time whilst getting my hair cut, Leamsi related to me the events that led him to end up in *The Big Tiger*. He had been running a little business in Nontha Buri district in Bangkok, a gambling racket. These little dens of iniquity were quite common in Thailand. Not only did the police tolerate them, they also frequented and protected them. As long as the police got their percentage, they could operate freely without fear of competition or raids.

However, the local police got greedy in Leamsi's case, and decided to increase the monthly payments. Leamsi got sick of this, and argued with one of the officers who came to collect the increased rates. The next night a dozen policemen raided his gambling den. Leamsi grabbed a few handfuls of cash, stuck a revolver in his belt and legged it out the back door. The police were gaining on him, so Leamsi fired a warning shot into the night sky and managed to get away. The following morning's newspaper carried a picture of Leamsi, accusing him of the murder of the son of the Nontha Buri police chief, who had been shot through the forehead in the chase. Leamsi maintained that he had shot into the air and that someone had misused the situation to murder the chief's son.

He knew that he would have to get out of Bangkok, and tried to board a bus going north to his family, but before he even got on the bus he was nabbed by a couple of plain-clothes cops and taken to Nontha Buri police lock up, where he was beaten so savagely he thought his number was up. During the beating he passed out, only to wake up in a pool of blood. His jaw was smashed, his ribs were broken, and a lung was punctured. The chief of police, whose son had been murdered, came down to the cell, put his heavy boot on Leamsi's already broken jaw, and hissed, "You are going to fucking die scumbag! Whatever it takes, I am going to kill you!."

Leamsi was sentenced to execution by firing squad. Nine years had passed since then.

41

GURU

I REALLY BEGAN to hit it off with Leamsi, who, believe it or not, had also been a junkie. He reckoned he could help me stay away from the gear. The magical quality I had seen in the monks on the island seemed to also be present in him, with his vibrant, chirpy demeanour, always patient and gentle with everyone he met. I asked him about this lucent brightness that he had, and he explained that he maintained his focus and awareness by meditating every day. After relating my experience with the monks to him, he went on to tell me a little story explaining this indefinable quality of mindfulness that is a by-product of meditation.

King Ashoka was the one who first made *Buddhism* popular in India a couple of thousand years ago. After a long and savage battle against a rival army, the King surveyed his victory, engulfed in grief as he stood among the wounded and dying soldiers from both armies, feeling their anguish. It touched his heart as he took account of the cost in human suffering and sacrifice taken to win him this victory. A *Buddhist* monk walked towards the King, dressed in a simple robe, barefoot and thin. As the monk came closer, the King could see the light in the monk's eyes; they shone with a glowing lucid awareness. He was serene and in harmony. Peacefulness seemed to flow from his very being. The King realised that for all his power wealth and fame, he was not happy in his own skin. He wanted whatever it was that this monk had. This realisation led to him converting to *Buddhism*, and under his reign *Buddhism* spread throughout Asia.

I thought this was a wonderful story because it demonstrated to me that happiness was something palpable; that it could be worked at, that there was a path, a method to be followed to find some peace within. Not just the reliance on the grace of some supernatural cartoon God figure in the sky. The only contradictory thing about the story was that if King Ashoka was so overflowing with Buddha's compassion, why did he then force all his subjects to convert? Seemed to defeat the purpose.

One day Leamsi asked me if I would like to escape. We both knew it was impossible. There was one recent incident where seven prisoners had hijacked a garbage truck and were mown down by machine guns. There was a stairway that led directly from Leamsi's barbershop to the nearby Execution Yard, with a broom cupboard underneath the stairs. Leamsie opened the padlock and motioned me to follow him inside. I was a bit hesitant at first. If this was an escape tunnel, I imagined the machine gun toting guards waiting for us at the other end. Leamsi had fashioned himself a little meditation chamber inside the broom cupboard, with a little *Buddhist* altar and two meditation cushions. The room smelt sweet with incense. Leamsi told me that officer Sonchai had asked for special permission that the broom cupboard be turned into a meditation chamber. Leamsi and Sonchai sometimes meditated together. Saint and sinner!

Under Leamsi's tutelage, I began to spend more and more time in the broom cupboard. It was a haven of tranquility in the middle of a very noisy prison, although most of the time I had to meditate wearing earplugs to limit the noise. Not only was this place an escape from the squalid prison environment, but it also gave my mind a rest from the constant barrage of self-criticism. In meditation, I could transcend or suspend thought. Leamsi explained that I had been addicted to thinking, and that most of my thoughts were harmful to me. He instructed me to concentrate on my breath just as the monks had done. This took my focus away from all the guilt, fear and uncertainty eating away at my insides.

My meditation sessions became longer and longer. Lots of answers came to me in the silence. Instead of exhausting myself with the constant noise of my rational, judgmental mind, I learned to switch off. This wasn't escapism, because I gradually became much more focused and aware. My mind was less clouded with emotion. I was developing a calmer more settled demeanour.

One day I bribed a guard to let me into the death row exercise yard for a hair cut. Leamsi looked like he had seen a fucking ghost. His complexion was pale and he looked gaunt and thin. He had a look in his eyes of total defeat. Most people in *Bang Kwan* looked pretty vacant, but Leamsi was normally an exception. He didn't let anything get him down. Never had I seen him look so bad. I sat down in a chair and he began to cut my hair, but his mind wasn't on the job.

"What's wrong with you, Leamsi? You look fucked." The lights were on but there was nobody home.

"Longhyn," he squeaked.

"Who the fuck is Longhyn?"

He put an English language newspaper in my lap. The headline said that the new Thai Prime Minister had announced his Cabinet. The newly appointed Deputy Minister of the Interior was to be Longhyn. He was the ex-chief of police in the Nontha Buri district. The guy whose son Leamsi was accused of murdering. The Thai correction department is a branch of the Ministry of the Interior. So Leamsi was resigned to the fact that he was going to die. The King had put a stay on executions, and for the past nine years, no one had been executed. I tried to reassure Leamsi that even if Longhyn wanted him dead he couldn't carry it out. But there was no talking to Leamsi, he was convinced his fate was sealed. After that he gave up on his commercial enterprises and began chanting and praying to prepare himself for the afterlife, with the help of Sonchai, the *Buddhist* guard.

Every day for the past five years the whistle blew at four o'clock as a signal for the prisoners to go back to their cells. One day the whistle blew at three. The guards started whacking prisoners with sticks, shouting at them to get back to their cells quickly. As I was pushed past death row I could see Leamsi sitting on the ground in a meditation pose, chanting. Then I saw the *face of death* coming through the yard. It was Bunuh the executioner. Most Thai's faces are expressionless, but this guy's profession oozed from every pore.

The look he gave me as he walked past chilled my spine. Inside our cells we communicated with the death row inmates via an air pipe that connected our toilets. They confirmed it. The barber was to be shot. The whole prison was deathly silent. Leamsi had been a popular man, and a lot of people started praying for him. We waited and waited, but no shots rang out. Four o'clock passed, then five, then six, and by seven we were sure Leamsi had been granted a reprieve by the King. Prisoners had begun to talk again and the mood had lifted. Suddenly five shots rang out. We could barely recognise the inhuman screams that came from the throat of Leamsi.

"Kill me, you fuckers! Just kill me!"

Shots rang out again but Leamsi was still screaming. A lot of people were covering their ears. What the fuck were they doing to this man? I cowered in the corner. I couldn't bear to hear the ghoulish wailing of Leamsi begging for death. More and more shots rang out, and finally Leamsi was silent. I couldn't sleep that night. I kept seeing the face of Leamsi writhing in agony as the bullets slammed into his body.

Next morning at six o'clock when the cell doors were opened, we trooped out into the yard. Nobody knew for sure what had happened; obviously, something had gone terribly wrong. Sonchai signalled me to follow him. He took me to an empty room and told me to sit down. Choked with tears, he related to me the events of the previous day's execution. He wanted to resign, as had some of the other death row guards, but he had only a couple of years left until his pension, and as he had a large family to support, he would just have to stick it out, even though he was disgusted by what had happened.

Apparantly the new Deputy Minister had lobbied the King to have the stay on executions revoked. Sonchai said that at four o'clock Leamsi had been led into the execution yard and strapped to a wooden cross, crucifixion style. His ankles, wrists and torso were secured by leather straps and his back was to the machine gun, a *Lee Enfield 303* with a five-shot magazine. The *Enfield* was bolted to a tripod on the paving. The area is lined with sand bags and there is a viewing area with plastic chairs. A *Buddhist* monk gave Leamsi the last rights on the cross. The Deputy Minister Longhyn had made a special request to be present at the execution. The barber was chanting *Buddhist* prayers as he sweated in the sunlight strapped to the cross.

Everyone waited and waited, but apparently Longhyn had got stuck in traffic. The barber's only view was the brick wall a few feet in front of him. The terror began to set in. He begged for the welcome oblivion of the grave. Between prayers he called the name of Bunuh the executioner, asking him to get it over with. Sonchai wanted to tell him why they were waiting, but was restrained by his senior officers. Even the *Buddhist* monk made a plea to the senior officer to do something about the situation.

The rule book stated that once a prisoner had been secured, only a reprieve would allow them to be untied. No-one had been executed in nine years and nobody seemed too sure of the protocol. Leamsi's pleas for death seemed to come from the bottom of his soul. The *Buddhists* believe that the state of your mind when you die decides where you will end up. Leamsi was to die violently anyway and had prepared for this, but for him, to be lashed to the cross, sweating, screaming, and writhing in fear for hours was sure to condemn his soul to eternal damnation.

Just before seven o'clock Longhyn showed up, drunk. He carried with him a few bottles of *Mekong Whisky*, and sat down in the viewing area signalling for Bunuh to proceed. Between Bunuh and Leamsi there was a white sheet, marked by a yellow coloured dot to indicate the area of the prisoner's heart. In the three-hour wait for the Minister, the sheet had moved around a great deal by the wind. The first volley of shots completely missed the heart area and severed Leamsi's left arm, leaving his left hand hanging grotesquely from the strap, and no longer connected to his body. Twisting his torso and head around towards the sheet he again begged Bunuh to do it properly. Bunuh reloaded and fired another volley into Leamsi. Again he missed the heart area and severed the other arm. It took another two magazines before Leamsi's pitiful pleas for death ended. Bits of body and blood were splattered all over the area. The Minister seemed pleased with the result. He had been slugging neat whisky throughout the execution and offered a drink to the guards to celebrate a job well done. Nobody was thirsty.

When Leamsi's family tried to collect the body, the guards didn't want to hand it over, and told the family it had been cremated. The family were within their rights and insisted on taking the body. When they saw the mangled mess of the corpse, the family were so incensed they drove straight to the King's residence and demanded to talk to someone. They threatened to display the mangled corpse at the palace gates and call the newspapers.

They were given an audience with the King's personal secretary who inspected the body. The next morning the King declared an amnesty for all death row inmates. All future executions were to be authorised by him personally. It was the anniversary of his ascension to the throne. The leg irons were removed from the death row prisoners and they were moved to another building. There was however, no change in status for drug traffickers, so it looked like yours truly would be here for a wee bit longer.

There are *Ten Commandments* for executions in *Bang Kwan* prison. Before 1934, it was a simple beheading, but as that was considered a little too barbaric for some of the scum that were being chopped, they introduced a 9mm submachine gun. This gun was first used on September 12, 1935 and executed a total of 213 offenders up until 1997, when it was replaced by a 9mm *HK* submachine gun. The *Commandments* for execution were:

> 1. A correction officer reads an execution order to the offender.
>
> 2. The offender's identification files and related documents are examined.
>
> 3. The offender is given time to work on necessary activities concerning his property and related legal documents.

4. A priest or a monk performs religious ceremonies. This is subject to the offender's religion or beliefs.

5. A last meal is arranged for the offender.

6. The offender is then fastened to the execution cross with his face against the cross. Both of his hands are also fastened together and filled with flowers, joss sticks and a candle. This is to pay respect to the *Lord Buddha* and the spirits, as well as to his victims.

7. The target screen is placed one metre from the offender's back. It is targeted at the offender's heart. This screen is also used to prevent the executioner from seeing the offender. Then the machine gun is positioned four feet from the screen.

8. The executioner will pull the trigger after the red flag is signalled.

9. The execution committee will then examine the dead body. The committee consists of the Governor of Nontha Buri Province, the Warden of *Bang Kwan* Central Prison, a representative from the Department of Corrections, the Chief Public Prosecutor of Nontha Buri Province, The Chief of Police of Nontha Buri Province and a medical doctor.

10. Finally, an officer will take fingerprints from the dead body and keep them as evidence of the execution. This is to make sure that the dead body is the person who was sentenced to death.

42

DEAR SON

THE STAY ON executions didn't last long. There was constant bickering in parliament, and the executions started again a couple of months later. Of course, there were numerous arguments for and against the death penalty and how it was to be carried out. They had considered allowing the condemned man to choose the method, but the downside was that if they made the wrong choice they might regret it for the rest of their lives. The general consensus of opinion was that lethal injection would be the most humane way to 'murder' someone. I would imagine Bang Kwan style would be not to bother sterilizing the needle. Not that it would make much difference really, but it would be typical of these bastards to send you on your final journey with a case of HIV thrown in for good measure. Saint Peter might be a picky bastard and Heaven's probably got a door code: No junkies, poofs, blacks or AIDS infested scum allowed.

The problem with lethal injections, according to the Chief of Prisons, is the cost. He reckons 8,000 *Baht* is far too much to waste on a needle and suggests that the pre-1935 method of beheading by sword would shiver the timbers of the criminal classes and terrify them into becoming model citizens. The Chief says that his job is crime deterrence and not prisoner rehabilitation. No room for *bleeding heart liberals* in this neck of the woods.

I try not to think too much about all this crime and punishment business. Thoughts can consume a man in here, and if I get caught up in all this injustice bollocks it will drive me mad. Last week a police general was jailed for the murder of a Saudi Arabian woman and her baby son. It was a jewellery embezzlement case and the Judge gave him life. A Thai woman was caught in possession of the said jewellery; the police searched her home and found a huge cache of drugs. She was the wife of the executioner Bunuh, the one responsible for shooting Leamsi. Like I said, I try not to think about it too much. Thoughts can consume a man. At least I have my sanctuary, my refuge, my cupboard beneath the *Place to Relieve Suffering*. The jail gets more crowded all the time. There are now 23 people in our five by ten metre cell; too many of us to lie down all at once, so we sleep in shifts. We are locked down from four in the afternoon 'til six the next morning. The constant proximity and noise of the other prisoners is unbearable. The Thai prison population is now 250,000 but the prisons were built to hold just 90,000 prisoners. That works out at 0.83 metres of space per prisoner instead of the intended 7.5 metres per head. It's quite sad how we work out these little mathematical equations to show how hard done by we are, but believe me, there's fuck all else to do in here.

There is still hope. There is always hope. There is a prisoner exchange programme going ahead at the moment, and some American prisoners were transferred Stateside and then let out on parole a few months later. The British Government is a bit reluctant to join the programme at the moment, but that could change. And maybe fucking pigs could fly. The British Consulate contacted my parents when I was arrested and I received a letter from my father. I like to sit in my broom cupboard and read my letter over and over again.

Dear Son,
Your poor bloody mother is at her wit's end! How d'yi always manage to git yirsel in these situations. The news of your arrest has been on the local TV and all over the bliddy papers. I canna' walk doon the street without some eejit asking me how my laddie is. I know what they're bloody well thinking as well. 'The laddie with the drugs up his arse.' Ahm sure yir aware of what people in Dundee think o' men that shove things up their arses. I'll no say yi didna' have it coming t'ya. Hanging aboot with all those bliddy hoodlums. How could yi no be like normal laddies; find a job, get married and settle doon? Ye hud tae go galavanting roond the world like Jack the Lad. Now look what's happened!

Well I think I've said my piece son, and I want ye t'know that we're doing all we can tae help ye. I don't know if ye deserve it, but I already lost one son and I dinna want to loose another. I know ye blame yirsel fir Danny's death, but I think the time has come fir all of us tae let it go.

We have sent some money and your older brother Tony is trying to organize a trip to visit you. He is still working on the rigs but he is now an engineer and travels to a lot of different countries and he says he will come and see you as soon as he can.

Danny's wife Bella had a bairn, it was a wee laddie. She called him Danny. He's the dead spit o' his father. I had him oot in the back green with the gloves on, teaching him a few moves. He's a great wee fighter, tall and slim and fast on his feet. He seems to have potential; the only problem is that he's a southpaw jist like yirsel. I'm trying to change him at the moment. Maybe this time I can nip it in the bud and stop this one goin' against the grain. Life goes on son so don't give up hope. Keep yir guard up and yir chin tucked in and above all keep yir bliddy hot head screwed on, yi daft wee bugger.
Dad

My main objective for the time being is to eat humble pie and try to get through this living hell. If I can keep the monkey mind in check I can survive. The only thing left is my awareness, and if you really think about it that's all we ever have. Circumstances are always changing. If I rely on circumstances to make me happy I am going to be very disappointed. I know my situation is pretty dire at the moment but Leamsi was right; I can escape! Every day in meditation I escape to the land of no suffering, a land where fear cannot reach me. When my mind leaves behind this dark forest of delusion and rests in quiet contemplation of 'what is', I surrender to the moment. Then, and only then, am I truly free!

Lightning Source UK Ltd.
Milton Keynes UK
30 December 2009

148042UK00001B/47/P